INCOGNOLIO

A NOVEL BY

MICHAEL SUSSMAN

INCOGNOLIO

Publishing Services: AuthorImprints.com
Cover design by Juan Padrón.
Author photo by Guy Michel Telemaque.

ISBN: 978-0-9991312-1-3 (Paperback)
ISBN: 978-0-9991312-0-6 (eBook)

Published by Janx Press, Cambridge, MA.
www.MichaelSussmanBooks.com

For Choco & Snootch

To Ann,
Unravel the
Mystery!
Wonderful seeing
you at Thanksgiving

There are three rules for writing a novel.
Unfortunately, no one knows what they are.

—W. Somerset Maugham

INSIDE

CHAPTER ONE

CHURN THE WEASEL

INCOGNOLIO.

Ever since the concussion, I can't get the damn word out of my head.

I haven't a clue what it means. But I love the *sound* of it. So, I'll make it the title of my novel and allow the entire story to spring forth from this mysterious word.

My neurosurgeon, Dr. Noggin, isn't so optimistic.

"Given the acute injury to your brain," he told me, "the resulting deficits in planning and organization don't lend themselves to the construction of an orderly plot."

Screw Noggin. If I wanted an orderly plot I'd reserve one at the cemetery.

The best tack, I decide, is to allow my compromised gray matter to dream up the tale as I go along, placing trust in my pinwheeling subconscious mind.

1

But where to begin?

In the past, I've found creative inspiration in simply walking the streets of the city. Not knowing what weather awaits me, I throw on a jacket, say goodbye to sweet Yiddle, scamper down as many steps as I see fit to create for myself, and emerge onto the busy street, which I've named Random Road.

As I head east toward the harbor, the brisk morning air clears my head, and it occurs to me that I've forgotten my janx. But I decide not to go back for it, for the simple reason that I'm not entirely certain what a janx is, the tendency to make up words being yet another symptom of my recent calamity.

After strolling a block and a half I spot conjoined twins standing in front of a brick building, begging for change. They're male, about twelve years old, each with just one arm and one leg to call his own. The onrush of people, bound as they are for important meetings and pressing engagements, fills me with shame for the way they casually ignore the twins.

The boy on the left has a gentle face, almost feminine in its features, and he brandishes an upturned newsboy cap. I retrieve a handful of change from my coat pocket—perhaps two or three bucks—and drop it in the cap. Lefty smiles radiantly and says, "Bless you, sir."

Righty, whose face is mean and insolent, scowls and says, "Cheapskate! How 'bout some damn bills?"

So I delve into my wallet, finding to my curious astonishment that it contains only rubles. With a shrug of my shoulders and an apologetic smile, I deposit a crisp hundred-ruble bill into the cap.

"What the hell's *that?*" says Righty.

"Sorry, it's all I've got."

"That's cool, mister." Lefty winks. "Have a grand day!"

"Asswipe," mutters Righty, and he spits at me.

Wiping the spittle from my brow with a monogrammed hanky whose provenance I couldn't trace if I tried, I forge onward. Two vicious Dobermans materialize at the ends of their leashes, snapping at me, reined in by an elderly woman dressed in a ratty bathrobe. Which reminds me to pick up some food for Yiddle, although now I'm pressed to recall whether I made her a dog or a cat—or even a goddamn parrot—and the absurdity of this budding saga gives me a sudden hankering for whiskey.

I'm on the verge of entering a bar when a kind-faced man dressed in an Armani suit pulls up to the curb in a Lamborghini convertible. He leans toward me and speaks. He's new to town and looking for the Khadaar. Do I know the way? I don't. In fact, I have no idea what he's talking about. But I've always wanted to ride in a

Lamborghini, so I say, "I'll take you there," and am invited into the passenger seat, whose soft leather feels like a cloud in heaven.

The driver introduces himself as Ko and I give my name as Muldoon. As the vehicle glides into traffic, Ko admits he had a hunch I knew about Khadaar. I smile knowingly, secretly wondering how I'll possibly direct him there, telling him, for no reason in the world, to take a left on Arbitrary Avenue.

When Ko inquires what level I've achieved, I frown, compelling him to elaborate.

"*You* know," he says. "What level of Incognolio?"

My heart quickens, for I feel instantly lucky to have stumbled upon someone who is familiar with the term. But then I realize that since I'm the one writing the story, it isn't luck at all. Furthermore, I wonder whether I might have created more suspense by placing a series of obstacles along the way.

It's too late now; the man in the driver's seat discloses that he has attained Level Six. I raise my eyebrows as if to convey a measure of being duly impressed, and just then I spot the sign for Destination Drive.

As I direct Ko to hang a right, he lets out a hoot and points to the Khadaar, a strange edifice that looks like a cross between a White Castle, a Shinto temple, and something else I'll think of later.

Ko parks the Lamborghini, and when the two of us pass through the entrance to the Khadaar, a young woman asks me to please remove my shoes. Reluctantly, I comply; my mismatched socks have holes, and now my big toes peek out. I survey the interior of the room, which is nondescript, since I remain torn between lavish and minimal decor.

My driving companion warmly embraces a tall bearded man, causing me to wonder if they are long-lost friends, while I amble to the end of the antechamber, where people pass through a purple velvet curtain into a sort of inner sanctum. Just as I reach the curtain, I'm distracted by a burning need to pee. I rise from my desk, my back stiff from sitting too long, and make my way through the apartment to the bathroom, where I urinate standing up, erasing any doubt that I am indeed of the male persuasion.

Glancing up from washing my hands, I'm startled to see that I cast no reflection in the mirror, which makes perfect sense since I've yet to describe what I look like. Not that I'd be caught dead doing so at this juncture, knowing full well that every amateur novelist and his sister uses the mirror as a vehicle for slipping in a visual description of the main character. Plus, what's wrong with letting you, the reader, use your imagination? Do I have to do *all* the heavy lifting? Hell, even the great

Voltaire believed that the best books were those in which readers themselves composed half.

So I facelessly dry my hands and return to my desk, and just as I'm about to revive the scene in the Khadaar, my phone rings and a charming female voice introduces itself as Delphia. She tells me she's got information that can help me find what I'm looking for and to meet her in twenty minutes at Hrabal's Tavern, just ten blocks away in Circle Square.

I put on a gray trench coat, which strikes me as appropriate since this is feeling more and more like a detective novel. But before I leave I remember to feed Yiddle, who turns out to be a parrot after all—an African Grey—and Yiddle squawks, *Better watch out, better watch out*, which sends a shiver down my spine because Yiddle is rarely wrong. Once outside, I follow Random Road west all the way to Circle Square, enter Hrabal's, and take a seat at the polished mahogany bar at which I've sat on many a long night, drinking myself into oblivion.

Hrabal limps over and pours me the usual, Jack Daniel's on the rocks, and shoots the breeze until he is distracted by a stylish woman who appears at the door. She's a luscious lass, just my type. Her leonine green eyes lock onto mine as she slinks toward me and parks herself on the adjacent stool. She orders a dry martini from Hrabal and turns to me. "I know about your quest for Incognolio."

For the moment, though, entranced by the exotic scent emanating from this luminous creature, I'm less interested in Incognolio than in Delphia and am scheming how to seduce her when I recall that a certain sad side effect of my concussion appears to be impotence. So, reluctantly, I set aside my amorous designs and ask her what she knows about Incognolio.

Delphia sips her martini and scrutinizes me. Seeming to come to a decision, she leads me over to a booth with a come-hither look and sits across from me. "Operation Incognolio," she explains, "is a covert CIA investigation of a strange phenomenon occurring at random localities in which the inhabitants gradually lose the ability to think rationally."

"Why are you telling me this?" I ask, adding that she must know I was placed on unpaid leave from the CIA after single-handedly botching Operation Pandemonium, mangling my prefrontal cortex in the process.

"Yes, Muldoon," she says. "I know all about you, including the novel that you're writing, the one titled *Incognolio*. That's why I got in touch. Even with your considerable cognitive impairment, I believe you are still the best damn detective around."

I eye Delphia suspiciously. "How do you know so much about me?"

"Because I possess the Faloosh," she replies, employing what is in all likelihood another of my made-up words. "It enables me to intuit the entire backstory of any novel in which I appear as a character."

I sit there stunned, gawking at Delphia, the first character I've ever created who is self-aware.

Once this revelation has sunk in, I ask her to tell me more.

"Incognolio is spreading through my hometown, where both of my parents are paralyzed by a total inability to follow a logical train of thought." Delphia looks deeply into my eyes. "I need you to help me discover the source of the epidemic in Whimsy."

Given my own aversion to lucidity, I imagine that an inability to cogitate would come as something of a relief. But Delphia looks distraught, so I agree to go visit her parents and see if I can help get to the bottom of their affliction.

I settle the tab with Hrabal and light out for Whimsy in Delphia's car, a brilliant red Ferrari. Before I know it, the two of us are sitting on her parents' sofa, drinking chamomile tea and trying to hold a semblance of a conversation with Mr. and Mrs. Yankerhausen. This proves a challenge.

For instance, when I ask Mr. Yankerhausen when he first noticed a shift in his thinking, he replies, "It was around the time that the kettle went to sleep, that is to say before the orange crimes revealed their cowboy addiction, festering in a kind of flaccid rotation of rejected noodles, the simpering fools having forgotten to release their canopies into the lagoon."

And likewise, when I ask Mrs. Yankerhausen whether she understood what her husband just said, she tells me, "Well, dear, at first it kind of went in one ear and out the cranberry valve, so I tried to belittle his noose, the poor snub, though I can't seem to fiddle the craw."

The entire interview proceeds in this fashion, while Delphia sits there in tears, and my own thought processes begin to churn the weasel. Then my phone rings.

It isn't my cell phone but the landline in my study. I stop typing and answer the call, which is from my literary agent, Myrtle Grouse, who has been a thorn in my side from the start.

"When are you sending me *Incognolio*?" she asks.

"Any day now," I reply, which is the sort of thing I've been telling her for nearly three years, since the publication of my last book.

"You're skating on thin ice, mister," says Myrtle, her way of reminding me for the umpteenth time that *Under Milquetoast* and *As I Lay Decomposing* have both gone out of print. "You have exactly three weeks to finish the thing or I'm cutting you loose."

This prospect sounds delightful except that, given my middling record of book sales, I'm unlikely to find

another agent, and this at a time when most publishers
won't even piss on an unagented manuscript, on fire
or otherwise. Were my monthly disability checks much
larger or my expenses much lower, I could afford to
tell Myrtle to take a flying leap, but since that is not
the case, I can't risk burning this bridge just yet, which
leaves me with no other choice than to mumble, "Yes,
Myrtle."

"And listen, Muldoon," adds Myrtle as a parting
shot. "If you want to get anywhere with this story, lose
the self-referential shtick. Metafiction is *so* played out."

Her words hurt, since I thought I'd made it apparent that this is a *parody* of metafiction. Nevertheless,
I grudgingly admit that it might make the manuscript
tougher to sell and agree to keep the self-consciousness
to a minimum. So as I hang up the phone, rather than
note that this might be a good place to wrap up the
opening chapter, I simply end it.

CHAPTER TWO

DETERMINATOR

I'm poised to pass through a purple curtain into the Khadaar's inner sanctum when a burly man with a thick beard hiding the lower half of his face and cryptic tattoos decorating his forearms puts a hand to my chest, halting me.

"What level are you?" he asks.

"Actually, I'm new to the Khadaar."

"No entry, sir. You must register with the Kajoob."

I'm trying to decide whether that's one of my neologisms or an actual thing when Yiddle squawks, *Get the mail, get the mail,* and I stop typing because Yiddle is hardly ever wrong. Two seconds later, the doorbell rings. I head downstairs, and sure enough it's the postman.

He hands me some envelopes—several past-due bills—and a small brown box for which I sign. Heading back upstairs, I notice that the return address on the box reads *Incognolio Industries*.

Curious as to the contents of the parcel, I retrieve my box-cutter from a kitchen drawer and hastily slice through the packaging tape, cursing when I lacerate my left index finger in the process. After sucking the blood off, wrapping my finger with a paper towel, and securing it with a rubber band, I pour myself a cup of coffee, settle into the breakfast nook, and open the box.

It contains a black terrycloth headband with the word INCOGNOLIO printed in red. The enclosed correspondence is signed by J.R. Cosmipolitano—CEO of Incognolio Industries—who congratulates me for having been randomly chosen to be among the first to receive their newest product. The letter continues:

> **Like most individuals, you probably assign some value to your free will, believing that the ability to choose between different courses of action is essential to human liberty and dignity.**

> *But what if I were to tell you that free will is an illusion, a false sensation produced by the brain?*

> **Indeed, neuroscientists have demonstrated that our experience of free will amounts to nothing more than a figment of our imaginations, and that our so-called *choices* are determined solely**

by our experience of past events and the unconscious neural workings of our brain.

*Not only is the notion of free will illusory, it is the
single greatest source of human misery.*

Unlike every other animal on the planet, humans
are burdened by worries, doubts, and anxieties.
Only humans suffer from guilt, shame, and remorse. This emotional distress all stems from the
simple fallacy that we are in control of our actions.

By wearing the Determinator® headband, you can
rid yourself forever of the myth of free will, and
enjoy a blissful state of peace and serenity.

The letter goes on to explain that the headband's two
electrodes, powered by a double-A battery, direct a
weak electrical charge at targeted areas of the brain,
thereby disrupting all neural activity associated with
the human experience of free will.

I'm about to crumple up the letter when I notice
that Cosmipolitano offers me five thousand dollars per
month to wear the headband and promote the product.
Indeed, I discover a check for that amount in the box,
signed by J.R. himself.

Despite the bogus-sounding claims attached to the
device, it's not an offer I can handily refuse. Hell, with
that kind of money pouring in, I can fire Myrtle and take

my sweet-ass time with the novel, make it as self-reflec-
tive as I please, or even stop writing altogether and take
up badminton or glass blowing.

Ignoring Yiddle's raucous insistence that it's a *Big
mistake, big mistake,* I insert a double-A battery into the
contraption, switch it on, and slip the terrycloth band
over my head, with the word INCOGNOLIO facing
forward.

At first I feel nothing at all, other than a faint tingling on my scalp. After two minutes, I feel vindicated.
The whole thing's a scam, just as I suspected. But who
cares so long as the dinero keeps flowing?

Then an odd thing occurs. My hand reaches out for
the coffee cup and lifts it to my mouth, I feel warm
liquid coursing down my throat, and my hand returns
the cup to the table.

Normally I wouldn't think twice about taking a sip
of coffee. But in this case, I made no effort whatsoever
to do so; it simply *happened,* without any conscious vo-
lition on my part.

Even stranger: when I *try* to take another sip of coffee, nothing happens. I just sit there staring at the cup,
unable even to lift my arm.

I try to stand up, but my legs are having none of it.
It must be a trick, perhaps some form of hypnosis, but
the initial impression is that I no longer have control
over my actions.

Then it occurs to me: maybe I never did. Is the Determinator the real deal? Might it actually work as described?

When I try to remove the headband, I find myself instead reaching for the brown box and retrieving a stack of promotional cards, then walking over to the coat rack, donning my trench coat, and placing the cards in a pocket. I leave some fresh water for Yiddle and say, "I'll be back."

The parrot replies, *How can you be sure?*

Once outside, I feel like heading to Hrabal's for a drink but turn right instead, toward the harbor.

Loss of free will sucks, as far as I'm concerned. Rather than peace and serenity, what I'm experiencing is more along the lines of annoyance and bewilderment.

But what if I stop fighting it? Surrender my will and just go with the flow? If I make believe that I'm, say, watching a movie, perhaps I'll no longer feel conflicted. It seems worth a try, so I continue down the sidewalk, noting that everyone I pass stares at my forehead, no doubt wondering what the hell INCOGNOLIO means.

Here and there, scattered among the oncoming pedestrians, I notice strange brawny creatures with gargoyle faces. As they pass by, they snarl at me and make menacing gestures. Looking down, I see that the paper towel is no longer covering my injured finger and think that the gargoyles might be drawn to my clotted blood.

At a newsstand I see stacks of *The Informer*, whose headline reads: *Senate Committee Probes Pecker*. This is puzzling, until I recall that President Pecker is being investigated for yet another of his constitutional transgressions.

Upon reaching the harbor, I turn right on Bottomless Boulevard and approach the Five Seasons Hotel. As I pass the doorman I hand him a card from my pocket and find myself saying, "Try the Determinator!"

Proceeding down the boulevard, I glance over my shoulder and see one of the gargoyles rushing at me, grunting and growling. Just as it reaches out to grab me, I hear the front door of my apartment slam and wonder who on earth has the key to my place.

As I scramble to concoct a backstory for myself, thinking maybe it would be better to have a wife or a girlfriend rather than a damned parrot, a skinny, sullen-faced teenage boy enters the study, kicks off his sneakers, and throws himself onto my leather sofa.

He resembles me, this young man, even though I've yet to settle on what I look like. So I assume he's my son, Greazly. He drops an f-bomb and explains that he is here against his will, that his mom made him come over. This implies that I'm divorced, let's say from a domineering woman named Fannie Mae, and I apparently have a strained relationship with my 17-year-old son, a wise-assed knucklehead.

"Whatcha writing?" asks Greazly. "Another shit novel?"

"This one's going to be great. Even *you'll* like it."

"Yeah, right. What's it about?"

"You know I don't like to discuss works-in-progress. It's simply a comic novel that appears to write itself."

Greazly snickers. "Sounds retarded."

"Please don't use that word."

Yiddle squawks, *Retarded, retarded*, making me uneasy—since Yiddle is rarely wrong—and I begin to worry that the novel's not as good as I think.

I turn my attention back to Greazly and ask about his day. He replies that he's been suspended until Monday, which compels me to sigh. "What happened this time?"

"My science teacher, Mr. Pecho, is a closet Creationist. He's always slipping in subtle digs at the validity of evolutionary theory." Greazly goes on to describe how he suggested that Mr. Pecho himself was living proof of evolution in a missing-link sort of way—a remark that, despite the mirthful appreciation it elicited from his classmates, landed Greazly in the principal's office.

I offer my son the spiel about respecting his elders, but it comes off as half-hearted since secretly I'm proud of him for putting it to his dim-witted teacher.

Even this mild rebuke annoys Greazly.

"Stop trying to change me," he says. "Why can't you just accept me for who I am? Jesus, I don't go around trying to change *you*, do I?"

"Of course you do. At this very moment, you're trying to change me into someone who won't attempt to change you."

But Greazly isn't listening, he's texting.

"That had better not be your degenerate girlfriend," I say.

"Why the hell not?"

"You know very well that you're forbidden to contact Areola since she convinced you to have sex on that rollercoaster. You were arrested, for Pete's sake!"

"Screw you, old man." He grabs his sneakers and storms out the front door, slamming it behind him, while I sit here feeling like a complete failure as a parent.

I'm just about to chase after him when it occurs to me that every time I leave my apartment it turns into another damn subplot. And since I'm already juggling the cult, the epidemic, and the headband, I opt to forego a fourth and instead call Fannie Mae to inform her that Greazly is on the loose and I'm in no position to pursue him.

She responds by yelling at me for nearly half an hour about my pathetic inadequacies as a parent, ex-husband, novelist, and human being. She takes pains to mention my small penis, which, even if it is small is certainly not *tiny*. Let's just say it's nothing to write home about. Not that you'd write home about a *large* penis, I suppose, the whole topic of genitals being best left off the table when corresponding with one's parents.

After she hangs up on me I sit with a blank look on my nondescript face, feeling utterly defeated, wondering which of the three subplots to return to or whether I should perhaps start another project altogether because I can't seem to shake this whole self-referential thing, which now feels claustrophobic and fills me with such trepidation that I am unable to type another word.

CHAPTER THREE

JACK SPANIELS ON THE BRICKS

For the next few days I stare at a blank page, unable to summon the muse. It's as if my imagination has gone on strike and won't even come to the bargaining table.

Noise from the street distracts me, so I use ear plugs. The lure of the World Wide Web proves irresistible, so I cancel my internet subscription. The blinking cursor mocks me, relentlessly ticking off the wasted seconds, so I fiddle with the settings until I manage to still it. And still I remain stuck.

Late one afternoon, while sitting at my desk, I receive a call from Dick Fracken, a freelance ghostwriter who claims to have met with me.

"Okay, Muldoon," he says. "I've sent you the first fifty pages of *Incognolio*, and I wanna be paid the first installment pronto, as we agreed."

"I agreed to nothing of the sort," I reply, wondering whether I've missed something.

"Bullshit. You signed a contact."

Since I haven't got any better ideas, I decide to go with this new subplot and see where it lands me. "A contract my lawyer informs me is highly irregular," I reply, warming up to my role, "and won't stand up in court. I succumbed to your persuasion in a moment of weakness, Fracken, but now I've regained my confidence and am writing the thing myself."

"Listen, you dickwad," says Fracken. "If you renege, I'm going to finish the damn novel and sell it under *my* name. Same title, same meandering form, same moronic sensibility. And believe me, after thirty years in the biz, I can crank out this dreck like diarrhea. My book'll be on the shelves before you can say Incog-fucking-nolio."

I hang up on Fracken, pour myself a whiskey, and gaze out the bay window. Now the pressure's on big time. I'll have to write day and night, jettisoning all rumination and second-guessing. No more excuses for me, from now on I'm going to grind out the pages.

But as I knock back the last of my drink, I notice Delphia walking by, so I grab my coat and hasten out to the sidewalk. When I catch up with her, a bit winded, Delphia smiles. She gives me a peck on the cheek, which makes my heart flutter even though I know full well that she's a fictional character. When I inquire about her parents, Mr. and Mrs. Yankerhausen, Delphia tells me the Incognolio epidemic has moved out of Whimsy, and that her parents are largely back to normal, although they still blurt out the occasional nonsensical remark.

I'm pleased to hear this. But then Delphia's face darkens and she informs me that Incognolio will strike our unnamed city any minute now.

"How can you know that?" I ask.

"I have the Faloosh," she reminds me, "which enables me to not only know everything that's happened thus far in the story but also to see what lies ahead."

"How does that work?"

"Our conventional concept of linear time is an illusion created by the human brain. In reality, the past, present, and future exist simultaneously. So, in a sense, the completed novel already exists, permitting me brief glimpses of what is yet to come."

The two of us have been walking west on Random Road and are now passing Hrabal's Tavern, so it seems natural to enter the bar. We find a booth in the corner and order drinks, a Jack Spaniels on the bricks for me and a wet Martooni for Delphia, which makes it apparent that Incognolio has already begun to take effect.

When Hrabal limps back with our drinks, I ask him how he hurt his leg.

"It's an old battle injury from the Great War, or per-
humps the Pretty Good War, who nose?" He winks and
crackles, and as I watch Hrabal lump back to the barn
I feel my brain start to twitch, and it behooves harder
and hardier to thunk straight, or even to cognize the
diffidence tween strait and curved, and dull Telphia, "I
think Incognolio has begun to resuscitate the blowfish,
we're no longer making incense," and she tries to crank
the pickle, but it's hamstering her agility to blink na-
tionally.

We vamoosh from the taberna and scumper around,
fingering that maybe there are safe pumpkins or pockets
where the vast tentacles of Incognolio won't aggrieve
us. Out on the street it's bedhem and maylam, pimples
running around in a froozy, unable to excommunicate,
cars crooning up onto the sidewalk, police arresting
their mothers, the entire city agash in a mixology of
contusion.

It blows on like this for what feels like mountains,
until, reverting hum, we discover that as long as we remain in my coat closet, the two of us are able to think
normally—or semi-normally in my case, given the afore-
mentioned brain damage—although we must remain in
the dark because the light bulb is missing.

And it comes as such a relief to think straight, and
she smells so wonderful, and we're in such close quarters, rubbing up against each other, that I impulsively

kiss Delphia, her mouth so warm and welcoming, her breath so sweet. But when I slide my hand around to her soft derriere, she gently pushes me away.

"Muldoon, the entire city is threatened by Incognolio and it's up to the two of us to figure out what is causing the epidemic," she reminds me.

"Right," I say, and have just begun to brainstorm when we're disturbed by a loud buzzing sound, which turns out to be my alarm clock, and I find myself waking up in bed alone to face the disappointing possibility that I merely dreamed the part where I kissed Delphia.

After a quick breakfast, I'm back at my desk, where I discover that I did, in fact, write the closet scene, as well as the waking-up scene, and even this sitting-at-my-desk scene, so there's really nothing left but to continue typing, despite having no inkling as to how much longer I can sustain this dichotomy of embodying the role of both writer and protagonist before it becomes tiresome, and furthermore wondering whether we're already well beyond that point.

I decide to pick up the headband storyline where we left off, with the growling gargoyle lurching at me with outstretched claws. I'm about to scream when I realize that it's not a gargoyle at all, just the doorman from the Five Seasons Hotel chasing me down, holding his cap to his chest.

"Sir?" he sputters. "Didn't you see the article in to-day's *Informer?*"

"You mean the Pecker probe?"

"No, the exposé on the Determinator. It's not what you think."

"How so?"

"They say there's a computer chip embedded in the headband. Along with the two electrodes, this allows them to both control your actions and induce halluci-nations."

That would explain the gargoyles.

"But why? What's in it for Incognolio Industries?"

"That's a shell corporation, sir. A front for the NSA. They're targeting individuals considered subversive by the government and driving them to suicide. The cops say people with those headbands have been jumping off buildings, throwing themselves under trains, even setting themselves on fire."

Why, I wonder, would the NSA bother with the likes of me? Sure, my previous novels could be consid-ered subversive, but no one actually reads them. Never-theless, I'm going to need some help if I want to avoid killing myself.

"I can't take the headband off," I say. "Will you do it?"

"My pleasure," the doorman replies. But when he reaches for it, I find myself delivering a vicious karate chop to his arm and then kneeing him in the balls.

The doorman doubles over and I apologize profusely, but I'm already turning to continue along Bottomless Boulevard. The road has begun to descend, which is odd since it borders the sea.

Now a pack of gargoyles is after me, along with various other monstrosities—werewolves, centaurs, golems, and zombies. In a panic, I break into a run, aware that the boulevard is descending at an ever-increasing angle, until it's so steep that I can no longer maintain my balance. I fall to the ground, rolling head-over-heels, the howls and roars of the pursuing creatures echoing all around me.

Suddenly it's quiet. I find myself in freefall, toppling down a pitch black void like Alice down the rabbit hole, wondering whether I too will enjoy a soft landing or be extinguished with a mighty splat that gets written up as yet another Incognolio-related suicide.

CHAPTER FOUR

THE REVOLVING CEMETERY

The following morning, just as I've begun writing, Yiddle squawks *Shrink time, shrink time*, and I'm reminded that I must go to my appointment with Dr. Miranda.

I feed and water Yiddle, put on a yarmulke—my therapist being under the impression that I'm an observant Jew—and walk several blocks to the Medical Arts Building, where my therapist shares an office with another psychologist, Dr. Schmendrik.

I arrive a few minutes late to find the office door standing open. Once I've settled into the armchair across from the good doctor she mentions that she happened to see me riding in a Lamborghini down Arbitrary Avenue without a yarmulke. Deeply embarrassed, I am forced to reveal that I'm not Jewish. As I stuff the yarmulke into my pocket, Dr. Miranda wonders out loud what other aspects of my life I might be fabricating in therapy, and it is at this point that I admit that I'm not a gay brain surgeon who grew up as an orphan in Liverpool.

Here I drop the cockney accent and stereotypically gay mannerisms and explain how, as a writer, I have always been afraid that being psychoanalyzed would undermine my creativity. Dr. Miranda reassures me that many creative people share the same fear and that it generally proves groundless.

"But tell me," she adds. "Why do you bother to attend these sessions at all?"

"Fannie Mae. She insisted on including it in our divorce decree, hoping that it would improve my relationship with Greazly."

"Greazly?" Dr. Miranda cocks her head. "Who is Greazly?"

"Um … that would be my son."

Now Dr. Miranda seems miffed, for which I can hardly blame her, given that up to this point my representation of myself has been a total sham. I apologize for having wasted her time and start to leave, but she says, "Perhaps it hasn't been wasted after all. Maybe you're just frightened of opening up and needed all this time to begin trusting me."

This strikes me as true, so I sit back down. "Why do you think I'd go to such lengths to avoid introspection?" I ask.

"Perhaps something happened to you in the past that was so traumatic you're afraid to explore it."

I go silent for a spell, reluctant to talk about the thing I've kept inside all these years and wondering whether doing so would help or simply make things worse. Rather than prompting me to say anything, Dr. Miranda sits patiently, her eyes kind and compassionate.

I decide to take the leap and open up. "You know how I talk about going every week to the Revolving Cemetery to visit the grave of my Nana Nellie? Well, I was twisting the truth. In fact, I don't have a Nana Nellie."

"You don't?"

"No, I never even called my grandmother Nana. But I *do* go every week to the Revolving Cemetery. It's to visit the grave of my twin sister, whom I call Micaela, although she was never actually given a name because she was stillborn." At this point my eyes well up and my voice thickens. "*Stillborn* has always seemed to me a strange word, since you can't really be born if you're still. If the baby is still then it's dead, and you wouldn't say *deadborn*—that makes no sense. Only living creatures can be born. But that's what happened, she was deadborn." And then the tears start to flow because I've never told anyone about Micaela.

Dr. Miranda hands me a box of Kleenex. I hold the box like it's something precious, although I don't actually remove any tissues, I just keep bawling, wishing Dr. Miranda would give me a hug, even though I know therapists aren't supposed to hug their clients.

Now I wish that the phone would ring and find me at my desk, happily typing away, the therapist scene just another stupid subplot I've blundered into. But the phone doesn't ring. I'm stuck in Dr. Miranda's office, and I know that this is real, no story, and that sucks. But by the end of the session I'm feeling a little better, and since it's Wednesday, I take the #33 bus to the Revolving Cemetery.

It used to be an ordinary cemetery, but decades ago they ran out of space for new graves. Some genius had the bright idea of building what looks like an enormous Ferris wheel that slowly rotates twelve numbered platforms, each with its own expanse of plots.

I wait nearly ten minutes until Platform Seven comes around, hop onto the carefully manicured sod, and head to Micaela's grave.

It's a tiny affair that lies there all alone, since my parents are buried overseas. The miniature headstone simply reads *Beloved Daughter* and notes the year of her stillbirth. I place some white lilies in front of the stone and stand there, feeling the dull momentum of the slowly rising platform, taking in the ever-expanding view of the city, wondering how my life might have been different if I'd had a sister to play and fight with, to confide in as I grew older. Perhaps I wouldn't have been so lonely. Perhaps I might have understood females better. Perhaps I wouldn't be wracked with a guilt that I don't even comprehend.

Why should I feel guilty? There was nothing I could have done to save her. But I can't help wondering whether Micaela might have survived had she not been forced to share my mother's womb with me, an interloper consuming limited nutrients. Maybe I even mauled the poor girl to death, my mother having frequently reminisced about what a vigorous kicker I was.

Maybe on some level I feel responsible, a murderer before I drew my first breath and then confused by how my parents, bereft of their daughter, seemed to give my arrival a subdued reception. My mother was too depressed to adequately nurture an infant, which left me feeling unwanted and unloved, unable to trust another human to meet my needs. All of this makes me feel so overwhelmingly distraught that I wish I'd never opened up to Dr. Miranda and released such a can of worms.

But what's done is done, so I turn my back on the grave and walk away, years of practice enabling me to have timed the length of my visit so that Platform Seven is just reaching the ground. I step off and leave the cemetery. As I'm walking toward the bus stop, a young man in a purple hoodie pokes his head out of an alley and says, "Wanna buy some Ink?"

At first I wonder why there would be a black market for ink. Then—on a hunch—I ask him what he means, and he snickers and says, "Incognolio, of course. Everyone knows that." He sneaks glances up and down the street. "You interested?"

"How much?"

"Eighty bucks a hit."

I buy one, a round black pill with a gold dot in the center. I ask the guy what it's supposed to do, but he pockets the bills and scampers down the alley.

I continue to the bus stop, but I'm feeling pretty depressed after visiting Micaela, so just as I board the #33 bus, I pop the pill in my mouth.

I take a window seat halfway down the otherwise empty bus. As I ride along I'm feeling no effects whatsoever, but then I produce an enormous belch and feel as if I've been turned inside out and immersed in an inky nothingness, my own personal black hole, where I remain immobilized for an indeterminate amount of time, thinking, *What a huge waste of eighty bucks.*

CHAPTER FIVE

TITLE WAVE

Still stuck in this lightless singularity, I wonder how I could have been so stupid as to have ingested street drugs obtained from some guy in an alley, a pill containing who the hell knows what manner of compounds. This is evidence that I am backsliding yet again into self-destructive ways, fiddling around with my brain chemistry when my psyche is already fragile.

As my self-castigation nears the point of pleasure, there's a sudden explosion of light and I pop out of the singularity like a Jack-in-the-box, only to find myself back on the bus. In fact, we're on the same block as when I burped, which suggests the entire episode lasted only a few seconds.

But then I hear laughter coming from somewhere behind me, and when I look over my shoulder I see several teenagers at the back of the bus, which is odd because the bus contained no other passengers when I entered the singularity. As I puzzle over this discrepancy, we pass a bookstore called Title Wave, a business I've never seen before in all the years I've been riding the #33.

I yank the cord and the driver pulls over at the next stop. I thank her, get off the bus, and walk back to the bookstore, whose window is, to my amazement, chock full of copies of *Incognolio*, each book bearing a gold Pulitzer Prize sticker on the front of the jacket.

Wondering what the hell's going on, I enter the store and a young woman by the cash register greets me. I nod my head and, afraid she might recognize me and think me vain for being interested in my own book, pretend to browse, eventually making my way over to the display stand for *Incognolio* and picking up a copy. Sure enough, it's my novel. Flipping through the pages I see the early chapters: Churn the Weasel, Determinator, Jack Spaniels on the Bricks, The Revolving Cemetery, and so on, and I'm just about to skip ahead to chapters I've yet to write when I notice something odd about the display copies.

Not only is each cover slightly different—color scheme, font size, etc.—but each copy also appears to have a different page count. Some books are as thin as a novella while others are thick as *War and Peace*. When I examine them more closely I find that no two books have the same table of contents, making me wonder, among other things, how it could have won any sort of prize when each panel member must have read a different text.

Still, I'm eager to read the thing, so I select three copies—thin, medium, and thick—and bring them to the woman at the cash register, who smiles, rings me up, and says, "Incognolio is selling like chowcakes," a phrase I've never heard before. When I look inside my wallet and find several fifteen and twenty-five dollar bills, I begin to suspect that the Ink has somehow landed me in an alternate universe.

But it's not until I'm headed home on the bus that I realize that in this universe I no longer experience guilt or self-loathing, and I wonder whether I feel so good about myself because of the Pulitzer. That seems unlikely because in the past when I received any sort of award or public recognition it only made me feel more guilty, more hollow inside, and in general I was far more comfortable dealing with failure and public disgrace.

When I arrive home, I grab the mail and walk up to the second floor, where I find the door to my apartment unlocked. As soon as I enter, a German Shepherd rushes at me, leaps up and licks my face, and then I hear an unfamiliar woman's voice call out, "Is that you, Muldoon?" Maybe I'm married in this universe and that's why I feel good about myself. Now I'm eager to meet my wife, who says, "Down, Yiddle, get down," and, before I have a chance to get a good look at her, wraps me in a warm hug.

The stunning woman who stands before me is about my age and looks strangely familiar, although I'm certain I've never seen her before.

"Where have you been?" she asks.

I tell her I was visiting Micaela's grave, which prompts her to stare at me incredulously, before laughing and saying, "Very funny."

Unsure how to respond, I set down the three copies of *Incognolio* and nervously sift through the mail, several pieces of which are addressed to Micaela, and I am struck by the shocking realization that the woman standing before me is none other than my twin sister.

I tell Micaela that I need some whiskey and she replies that there's none in the house, since neither of us drink alcohol—a statement that obliterates any lingering doubts that I'm in an alternate universe.

I lead her into the living room and sit her down on a sofa made of cheese, or at least that's my initial impression, although it turns out to be some weird fabric that looks like cheese. The sofa reminds me that I haven't eaten all day, so Micaela dials a local restaurant and orders Vernulian—apparently my preferred cuisine in this neck of the woods—then listens to me talk of how a black and gold pill landed me in this universe, and how in my home universe Micaela was stillborn and I have mourned the loss by visiting her grave without fail every Wednesday my entire life, a life so filled with misery that I am an alcoholic who on several occasions has tried to kill himself.

At first Micaela chuckles, probably thinking this is another one of my pranks, but when she sees from my face that I'm serious, she lovingly strokes my hair and proceeds to grow tearful.

The food arrives, luscious pampanus and succulent makmaks, and eating puts both of us in a better mood. Later, as Micaela feeds Yiddle the leftovers, she tells me all about the wonderful life I've led in this universe, where I'm a wildly successful author and amateur bomb defuser, and how the two of us have remained so close that we recently decided to live together.

Fascinated by each other, we talk late into the night, as enthralled as new lovers. When we decide it's time for bed, while she takes a shower, I puzzle over the sleeping arrangements, having found that the second bedroom—Greazly's room in my home universe—has been turned into a meditation room.

Thoroughly confused, I go into my bedroom, and I'm sitting on the double bed when Micaela walks in, stark naked, her body in remarkable shape for a woman of forty-two. She leans down and kisses me full on the lips, and then she gently pushes me back onto the mattress and lies next to me, drawing little circles on my chest and gradually moving her caresses southward.

I snatch her hand just as it dips beneath the waistband of my trousers and ask what the hell she's doing. Micaela blushes and apologizes. Shocked and disgusted, I pull away from her and hold my head in my hands while she gets up and puts on a nightgown.

When Micaela returns to the bed, she takes a seat next to me and explains that this has been going on since we were teenagers. Although we've both taken other partners, we always seem to gravitate back to each other.

I describe how incest is viewed back home, and she laughs and says, "That's silly, what's wrong with it if we're careful to use birth control?"

This is more than I can handle for one day, so Micaela makes up a bed for me on the sofa and kisses me on the forehead. When she looks deep into my eyes, smiles, and says goodnight, I realize that I love her more than I've ever loved anyone in my entire life.

CHAPTER SIX

FLAWLESS
TOOTSIES

In the morning, I awaken in my own bed. Micaela is nowhere to be seen, the sofa no longer looks like cheese, and Yiddle is a parrot again. The Ink must have worn off.

Without Micaela there I feel empty, lonelier than I ever did before, and I curse the drug for having given me a glimpse of what might have been.

In thinking about the sexual relationship that I apparently share with my sister, I am filled with shame and revulsion. Secretly, though, I'm excited when I imagine it, almost wishing I hadn't turned her away when I had the chance.

When I'm feeling this low, I recall the writer's adage that you must stay drunk on writing so reality cannot destroy you. I sit down at my desk and am encouraged to note that I'm already forty-two pages into the manuscript. That's a good start, though I wish I'd read one of the published copies of the novel so I'd have some idea how to proceed.

It's been a while since we checked in on the Khadaar, so I reread the part in Chapter Two where I'm prevented from passing through the purple curtain into the inner sanctum by a burly man who says I must register with the Kajoob, and I pick up the scene at that point, finding my way downstairs and into the basement.

I am directed to a large waiting area in the back, where I take my seat along with seven or eight other people and wait for the Kajoob, who fails to appear, this for the simple reason that I've yet to form any image of him or her. Visualizing people used to come easily to me, but it's as if the concussion affected my so-called mind's eye and I have great difficulty forming any sort of internal image, as if I've become internally blind.

Every half hour or so, the Kajoob's assistant comes in, points to one of the people in the waiting room and escorts that person down the hall. It looks like I'm in for a long haul, without any magazines to kill the time, and I'm on the verge of getting up and going back home when a pretty young woman enters the waiting room and sits down next to me.

She's wearing a short skirt and strappy sandals, and I find myself stealing glances at her lovely feet, which are perfectly proportioned and meticulously pedicured, with turquoise nail polish and a tiny pink rose hand-painted on the nail of each big toe. Entranced by the sight of such flawless tootsies, I wonder whether she realizes how excited a man can get at the sight of her feet, as if she were sitting there in the waiting room with her bare breasts exposed.

"I see you like my feet," the woman says.

I look up at her as if I have no idea what she's talking about. "Oh, I was just admiring your sandals. I used to own a shoe store, you see, and I don't recognize that brand."

I introduce myself, she says her name is Arielle, and when I ask what she is doing here she lowers her voice and tells me that she's researching an article for the *Informer* on the Order of Khadaar.

I'm about to ask her what she knows about the group when the assistant enters and points to me, even though there are others who've been waiting longer. Though disappointed that my time with her has been cut short, I tell Arielle it was nice meeting her, steal one last look at her feet, and follow the assistant down the hall and into the office of the Kajoob.

The Kajoob greets me, and now I'm forced to come up with some sort of description, so I decide—or it

simply comes to me—that it's a he and he's a mysteri-
ous-looking gentleman in his sixties with a bald head,
unkempt gray beard, and wandering eyes that are cloud-
ed over, milky white.

The assistant leaves and I take a seat across the desk
from the Kajoob, who raises his palms toward me. It
feels like he's scanning me, reading my mind and emotional state, maybe even my aura if such a thing exists.

After a couple of minutes, he lowers his hands and
asks why I have attempted to take my own life. Disconcerted, I'm not sure at first how to respond, but finally tell him that I have a self-destructive streak and
that a part of me feels everyone would be better off if
I checked out.

"You cannot check out," the Kajoob replies, "since
consciousness never dies. But what if you could heal
these self-destructive tendencies and accept yourself as
you are? What if you could adopt a new way of viewing
yourself and the world, a revolutionary perspective that
would put an end to all suffering?"

"That sounds great," I say. "But I hope it doesn't involve putting my faith in some sort of deity, because I
find that stuff hard to swallow."

The Kajoob chuckles.

"Believers and nonbelievers alike are welcome. All
that is required is a willingness to open yourself to new
experiences."

This sounds reasonable, and I'm eager to know what Incognolio is, so I agree to join the Khadaar, wondering whether it will involve signing any papers or forking over any money. But the Kajoob merely tells me that I must journey by shuttle bus to the Compound, a rural commune where I will undergo a two-week Intensive and be initiated into the Order of Khadaar.

"If you hurry," he says, "you can catch the next shuttle."

"I'll have to go home first and pack some things."

"Not necessary. When you arrive at the Compound you will be supplied with clothing and toiletries."

I thank him and am headed back upstairs to catch the shuttle to enlightenment when I hear a tremendous crash that sounds like someone has busted through my front door.

A barrel-chested thug appears in the doorway to my study and comes at me in a threatening manner. I jump up out of my seat and say, "What the hell is going on?" and he sucker punches me in the gut. I stagger, trying to remain on my feet, and then he slugs me in the jaw and I collapse to the floor.

I lie there, stunned, as Yiddle squawks, *Gratuitous violence!*

The guy rolls me over, ties my hands behind my back, hauls me up to my feet, and throws me over his shoulder like a duffel bag, then carries me out of the

apartment and down the stairs before shoving me into
a panel van.

I roll helplessly around in the back of the vehicle for
what seems like forever, straining to remember whether
I have any enemies. He finally pulls to a stop and, from
the sound of it, closes a garage door. Then the door of
the van slides open and there's my answer, grinning at
me malevolently, that rat-faced, overpaid, scumbag of a
ghostwriter, Dick Fracken.

CHAPTER SEVEN

SMOTHERBOX

Now that I've kidnapped Muldoon, I can finally hijack the narration. And job one is to shorten the sentences. No run-ons for me. As the preeminent ghostwriter of trashy novels, I know as well as anyone that when it comes to sentences, less is more. The shorter the sentences, the greater the book sales. Chalk it up to laziness or short attention span, but it's that fucking simple. Why else are so many adults reading *young adult* novels?

I order Grunt to drag Muldoon out of the van, one of several vehicles parked in my oversized garage. On my command, Grunt manhandles the captive into my sprawling 12,000-square-foot mansion, an edifice worthy of *Homes of the Rich and Famous*. The three of us proceed to the cathedral-ceilinged living room, featuring a spectacular view of the open sea from its perch

atop a 500-foot cliff. The room is jam-packed with
world-class art—Pollack, Rothko, and Modigliani—and
furnished with the ultimate in Danish Modern design
pieces.

After untying Muldoon's hands, Grunt leaves, and
I offer Muldoon a seat. He stands and, after glaring at
me for several seconds, complies. I ring a hand bell and
Quenchley—my butler—appears, bearing pastries and
Earl Grey tea, which Muldoon refuses.

"Perhaps you'd prefer whiskey?" I say.

"I'll have you arrested for this, asshole," he replies.

"Good luck with that. Cops are in my pocket."

"So what the hell do you want from me?"

"Stop writing *Incognolio*."

"Think again," says Muldoon. "My agent set a deadline and I intend to meet it."

"Not if I keep you here."

"What's it to you, anyway? Isn't your latest Floyd
Robertson piece of shit selling well?"

"Number one on all the lists." I smile and sip my
tea. "As you can see, I've got plenty of dough. What I
don't have is fame and recognition. I'm the top-selling
novelist in the country, yet no one knows my goddamn
name."

"With a name like Dick Fracken you should count
that as a blessing."

I devour an éclair and suck my fingers clean.

"Enough small talk," I say. "Stop writing *Incognolio* and waive all rights to challenge my version in court— or we'll begin, ahem, enhanced interrogation."

"Go straight to hell, you hack."

"Have it your way." I blow a high-pitched gold whistle that hangs from my neck, and Grunt instantly appears.

"Take him below," I tell Grunt. "As you'll see, Muldoon, I have my own little version of Gitmo in the basement."

I give him time to sweat it out while I get a rubdown from Malena, my Swedish masseuse. After my happy ending, I go below and join Grunt and Muldoon. The latter's face has turned ashen.

"Impressive, isn't it?" I say, gesturing toward the extraordinary assortment of torture devices assembled in the room. There's an antique rack from the Tower of London, a pillory, and an iron maiden from the Ming Dynasty. There's a wooden horse, a Judas chair, a water board, a smotherbox, and all manner of thumbscrews and tongue shredders. Hanging from the walls are gags, whips, paddles, crops, cudgels, cattle prods, nipple clamps, and suspension cuffs.

Muldoon sits at a metal table in the center of the room. Lying before him are a pen and the contract I had my lawyer draw up.

"Sign it." I take a seat across from Muldoon. "Spare yourself the excruciating pain."

"Why do you even have all this stuff?" he asks. "Who do you use it on?"

"My authors," I reply. "Do you think I got this stinking rich on standard ghostwriting contracts? By the time I'm finished with my clients, they're lucky if they get any royalties at all."

"Well, do your best. You don't scare me."

"Oh, I have no intention of using any of these devices on you, Muldoon." I grin and crack my knuckles. "I happen to know that your pain tolerance is off the charts."

Muldoon stares at me grimly, straining to figure out my angle.

"No, you're a guilt and shame man," I say. "It's *emotional* pain that'll get me what I want from you."

Muldoon swallows hard.

"We both know that what little you've revealed about your backstory is bullshit. Well, I think it's time to set the reader straight."

Tiny beads of sweat appear on Muldoon's forehead.

"You're not married to Fannie Mae," I begin, "because you've never been able to sustain a love relationship. And you abandoned your teenage son at an early age and have ignored his recent attempts to renew contact."

Muldoon's left eye begins to twitch.

"Furthermore, you're not brain-damaged, you're mentally ill. You've been in and out of psychiatric wards and receive disability payments due to manic-depression with episodes of psychosis."

There goes the right eye.

"You have no literary agent and your previous novels, *Under Milquetoast* and *As I Lay Decomposing* remain unpublished. You're a madman who imagines himself a writer in order to give yourself a reason to live."

Now sweating profusely, Muldoon presses his eyelids shut.

"And then there's this." I remove a piece of paper from my pocket and unfold it. "Public intoxication. Vagrancy. Trespassing. Disturbing the peace. Resisting arrest. Possession of psychedelics. Possession of narcotics. Three DWIs. Driving without a license."

Muldoon hangs his head. The end is near.

"Oh, and let's not forget about Micaela." Muldoon looks up, his eyes filled with dread. "She wasn't stillborn, was she? That's merely what you tell yourself to avoid facing the fact that you killed her when she was only—"

"Enough!" cries Muldoon. "I'll sign."

"Not so fast." I grab the pen. Having triumphed much more easily over Muldoon than I'd anticipated, a new idea occurs to me. I have an opportunity here to take on all of the glory and none of the pain. "I've de-cided that your questionable writing style and twisted imagination are well-suited to an anti-novel like *Incog-nolio*."

"What are you saying?"

"At this point, I couldn't care less about royalties. You take 'em. But when you finish the novel, *my* name goes on the cover."

A broken Muldoon weakly nods his head.

"Excellent. I'll have my lawyer draw up the new contract," I say. "From here on in, Muldoon, *you're* the ghostwriter."

CHAPTER EIGHT

RAZA LARAT

Soon I'm back home, disgusted with myself for allowing that bastard to reveal my true background, the details of which are enough to turn anyone still reading this novel against me, not to mention that I'm now obligated to complete a book for which I'll receive no official credit.

It's time to face the music and admit that I'm a pathological liar who slanted and fabricated much of the earlier material in an effort to win the reader's sympathy. The upside being, this leaves me with no choice but to overcome my shame and guilt, stop running from my past, and find a way to write authentically.

It means learning to write for myself, not to please readers or to make it onto a bestseller list. What's important is not who takes credit for the work, but that the novel be a vehicle for coming to terms with myself and discovering the meaning of Incognolio, which I am convinced holds the key to everything.

I knock back two shots of whiskey, sit down at my desk, and return to the cult story, in which I complete the four-hour bus ride from the Khadaar to the Compound. On our arrival, the other novices and I are separated by gender and escorted to a commissary. We're told to strip and hand over all our clothing and possessions to be stored away in baskets, then given white cotton yoga-style pants and shirt, underwear, toothbrush and toothpaste, a brown bar of soap, and a thread-bare towel.

Then we're led to a bunkhouse, where I choose a top bunk and dump the toiletries atop a stained and scratchy-looking wool blanket, after which I follow the others to the dining hall for a dinner—which we are requested to eat in silence—consisting of plain yogurt, brown rice, herb tea, and a Ding Dong for dessert.

After dinner, there's a welcoming ceremony in the Hall of Miracles for the three dozen or so novices, culminating in an address by Babaganu—the founder of the Order of Khadaar—who sits lotus-style on a purple pillow, a sparkle in his eyes and an enlightened smile on his face.

Babaganu greets everyone and goes on to say that several years ago he was depressed and suicidal, having bankrupted his Fortune 500 company, which cost him his wife, friends, and all his money, and just as he was about to leap off Preposterous Tower, the tallest sky-scraper in the city, a word flashed through his mind: Incognolio.

"I know that doesn't sound like a profound reve-lation." Babaganu grins. "Merely a nonsense word and nothing more. But in that moment of crisis it saved my life. The veil of illusion fell away and I stood face to face with the Mystery of Creation, the Great Unknown, filled with a transformative sense of joy and peace."

Babaganu takes a deep breath, slowly releasing it through his mouth.

"Incognolio can save your lives, too. It can lead you step by step to a state of illuminated consciousness, true enlightenment, in which you are released from all suf-fering and brought into harmony with the entire cos-mos.

"But simply hearing the word isn't enough. And that's the reason for this two-week Intensive. It is less a meditation retreat than a spiritual boot camp, an ordeal in which you shall be subjected to severe stress and tor-ment, producing a state of heightened awareness and an attitude of surrender—akin to my own state of mind as I looked down from the tower—priming you to receive the full blessings of Incognolio."

When the meeting ends, I make eye contact with Arielle—the journalist—who smiles at me. But we have no time to converse since everyone must prepare for bed, which turns out, beneath the blanket, to be a bed of nails, something I'd always thought was a legend. In any event, I sure as hell can't sleep on it, despite trying through the long night to find a sleeping position that doesn't entail unbearable pain.

At 5:00 A.M. my bunkmates and I are roused—although none of us were fully asleep—by an annoying screech that blares over the loudspeaker for several minutes. The lot of us are sent to clean the latrines, after which we dig ditches for an hour, followed by a silent breakfast of brown rice, herb tea, and a Ding Dong.

After the meal, everyone's head is shaved, including the women, and we are stripped down to our underwear. Then we are all herded out to the Rock Board, a field laid out like a giant checkerboard, with huge 30-pound rocks in place of checkers, and the novices are divided into two teams.

There are four referees, called savaks, who explain the rules of the game, which are so complicated that we have no idea what they're talking about. Then a starting gun is fired and each novice in turn must lift one of the rocks and haul it to a new space, which in itself is laborious work under a scorching sun.

Making matters worse is the fact that when someone makes an ill-advised move—which happens more or less constantly since no one understands the rules—the savaks assault the offending player. For instance, when I make my first move, hoisting my rock and lugging it two spaces forward, they converge on me and scream, "What an idiot, what a stupid move!" Getting right up in my face, they yell that I'm a worthless piece of shit and shove me until I fall to the ground and knock my head against the rock.

At one point, I find myself standing adjacent to Arielle while another player is beaten and humiliated.

"What do you know about this Babaganu?" I whisper to her.

"His real name is Raza LaRat," Arielle replies. "He's a conman. Served time for drug smuggling, mail fraud, and racketeering."

After two hours of lugging the heavy rocks around and being brutally ridiculed by the savaks, many of the novices are dripping with sweat, severely sunburned, and in tears. When Arielle makes a bad move and the savaks whip her while calling her a filthy whore, I go berserk. I take out one of the savaks with a vicious kick to the groin and tackle another one. Two more of them subdue me, work me over, and drag me off of the Rock Board and throw me into a hotbox—a pit dug in the earth—then close and lock the lid, leaving me alone in the sweltering darkness.

CHAPTER NINE

CRIME AND PUNISHMENT

Sitting in total darkness and intolerable heat on a pile of what smells like rotting fish heads, my entire body throbbing from a sound pummeling, I think things can't possibly get any worse when they start piping in a zombie-like voice that drones:

HUB-ba-da, HUB-ba-da, HUB-ba-da, HUH.

HUB-ba-da, HUB-ba-da, HUB-ba-da, HO.

HUB-ba-da, HUB-ba-da, HUB-ba-da, YEE.

HUB-ba-da, HUB-ba-da, HUB-ba-da, YO.

The stench, heat, and mind-numbing chant hinder my ability to think. But there's nothing else for me to do, so I ponder my situation as best I can, wondering how long they'll leave me here, what other ordeals I'll be subjected to, whether Arielle and I can figure out how to get past the electrified fences, and occasionally recalling how great Arielle looked in her underwear.

After an unknowable period of time spent in these conditions, I hear a woman's voice calling out my name—*Muldoon, Muldoon*—and I'm wondering if it's Arielle when I am startled by a hand lightly slapping my face. So I reach out in the darkness and feel the body of a woman sitting next to me, and when I ask who's there she says it's Delphia.

To my amazement, I'm no longer in the pit but back home in my coat closet, having discovered in Chapter Three that it's the one place where Delphia and I can think rationally, untouched by the Incognolio epidemic. I tell her that I have somehow managed to transport myself from the cult subplot to this epidemic subplot.

"Naturally." Delphia laughs. "After all, *you're* the one writing the novel."

I realize that she's right, that I've somehow lost my sense of agency within the narrative and repeatedly become ensnared in the productions of my own imagination: freefalling down Bottomless Boulevard, stuck in a closet, imprisoned in a hotbox.

"Are you saying that we can walk right out of this closet and think normally if I simply decide that the epidemic has moved out of town?" I ask Delphia.

"It's worth a try," she responds.

So I get up and open the door and the two of us walk out into the living room.

I turn to Delphia, who says, "Withered shots of horsemint have jammed my hackleberry doormat."

I frown and reply, "There are no brain feathers left in the humpmoose cataclysm."

Disapportioned, I grample her and brinkly scrunch back unto the closnet.

Once my head has cleared, I say, "See, it's not so simple."

"I guess not," Delphia replies. "Your subconscious mind has such a firm grip on the story that you're limited in the degree to which you can consciously direct the plot."

"What about the Faloosh? Can you use it to see into the future and find out how we solve the mystery of the epidemic?"

"Afraid not," says Delphia. "The Faloosh grants me visions spontaneously and can't be willed."

I sigh. "I guess we're stuck in the closet, for now."

"Unless..."

"Unless what?"

"Why don't you just stop writing and find yourself back at your desk? Then you can go see your therapist and try to figure out how to proceed."

That sounds like as good a plan as any, so I close my eyes and when I open them again I find myself at my computer, typing out this sentence.

I call Dr. Miranda, and although I'm not scheduled to see her until next week, she says to come right over because her 2:00 P.M. cancelled. When the unsolicited input I'm expecting from Yiddle doesn't arrive, I decide to give her some much-needed attention. I gently stroke her and whisper what a good bird she is, and then walk down Random Road to my therapist's office.

I've been emailing my new chapters to Dr. Miranda—the only person I dare show them to—so she's aware of how the story is progressing, or regressing as the case may be. "I feel I've lost my way," I tell her. "I have no idea where the story is headed, and I seem to be fighting my own subconscious, making it increasingly difficult to write."

"Tell me," says Dr. Miranda. "How would you distill the novel down to a single sentence?"

I think it over and say, "It's the story of a man who tries to liberate himself by writing a novel in which he gives his subconscious mind free rein. At least that was the idea when I started the thing. But the deeper we get into the story, the more disturbed my protagonist seems to grow."

"Yes, I can see that. But perhaps it's like the process of psychotherapy, in which people often find they become *more* distressed and may even feel themselves falling apart before things begin to get better."

"That's all well and good, but at least in therapy everything I say remains confidential. A novel can be read by anyone who buys, borrows, or steals it."

"True," says the doctor. "Maybe you're feeling blocked because you fear that giving your subconscious so much leeway is dangerous. That your writing may reveal material that is threatening to you and that you may not want to share with others."

"Exactly," I reply. "I'm broke and intent on writing a book that will earn some serious scratch, but most of the reading public simply want to be entertained, not challenged by the ravings of a certified lunatic."

Dr. Miranda shakes her head. "It's possible you are using this rationalization to hold yourself back from doing some real digging. Many of the great works of literature are about precisely that, delving into the deranged mind of a character who exists beyond the pale."

I'm in no danger of writing a classic. Still, the doctor makes a good point. And when I take into account the fact that Fracken's name—not mine—will appear on the book cover, ruling out public humiliation as a demotivating factor, the only logical conclusion is that I'm struggling with the story because I fear stumbling upon something that threatens my psychological stability. My choice is between courageously forging ahead and giving up writing altogether.

"Perhaps what's gumming up the works," Dr. Miranda suggests, "is that you've yet to confront—either in therapy or in your manuscript—what Dick Fracken revealed in Chapter Six, which is that Micaela did not die at birth. The truth of the matter is that you killed her."

"Where does the time go?" I say, getting up to leave.

"We still have twenty minutes." Dr. Miranda smiles.

I sigh and reluctantly sit back down. I'm scared stiff of this topic—talk about a can of worms—but maybe ultimately it will do me good to get the story off my chest, and it might jump-start my writing to boot.

"As you know," I tell Dr. Miranda, "I am extremely guarded and secretive, prone to hiding my thoughts and feelings from others, if necessary resorting to deception, distortion, and outright lies in order to conceal my true self. This trait accounts for my abbreviated relationships with women, who tend to desire a level of honesty that I'm unwilling or unable to provide.

"Although we were fraternal—not identical—twins, Micaela and I shared an intimate bond and were pretty much always on the same wavelength. She was so sensitive and intuitive that she knew precisely what I was thinking and feeling at all times. At first it felt comforting to be understood so completely, but by the time I was seven it had begun to feel intrusive and suffocating.

"Looking back on it, I responded by detaching from my feelings and becoming so alienated from my own self that I no longer felt connected to her. But this disengagement was never complete, and the farther I drew away from her—and from my true self—the harder Micaela pushed to break through my barriers."

"Tell me how Micaela died, Muldoon."

"I never meant to kill her! I just wanted to scare her so badly that she'd back off and leave me alone." I take a shaky breath and forge ahead with my tale.

"I'd been considering various options for several weeks, when an opportunity presented itself. We were riding on the giant Ferris wheel at the amusement park one summer evening, and just as our gondola reached its zenith, there was a sudden jolt and the Ferris wheel screeched to a halt. Recognizing the opportunity for what it was, I grabbed Micaela and made as if to push her off, at which point she looked at me, dead serious, and said, 'I know you want to kill me.' This made me so furious that I actually wrestled her out of her seat and dangled her over the edge of the gondola."

My mouth is dry as dust and my voice cracks as I describe Micaela's screams and how people on the ground pointed up at us as I tried to pull her back to safety.

"But I wasn't strong enough. I could only hold onto her hands and peer into her terrified eyes. We both started weeping. Finally, after what felt like ages, a fire truck appeared and a fireman started ascending in a cherry-picker bucket. But the thing was too damn slow. The fireman was saying, 'Just hold on, boy, hold on,' but my shoulder muscles were blazing with pain. I reached the point where I knew it was over. I told Micaela I loved her, and she slipped from my fingers and plunged to her death."

CHAPTER TEN

PLATFORM SEVEN

I had hoped to feel some sense of relief after divulging my long-buried secret, but instead I feel empty and numb. So after bidding Dr. Miranda goodbye, even though it isn't a Wednesday I decide to go visit Micaela, hoping to break through my stupor.

Taking the #33 bus to the cemetery as usual, I step onto Platform Seven and remember my first encounter with the graveyard after it had been converted into the Revolving Cemetery. I recall how mortified I was, convinced they were deliberately mocking Micaela's death by building a cemetery that bore such an uncanny resemblance to the very means of her death.

I place my bouquet of white lilies against the headstone and stare down at my sister's grave, feeling detached as the platform slowly rises. Just as it reaches the top, I notice dark storm clouds rolling in toward the city. Then there's a grating metallic sound, and the platform shudders and comes to a stop.

This has never happened before. I chalk it up to synchronicity—since it seems like such a stupendous coincidence that I should become stuck on the Revolving Cemetery on the very afternoon that I disclose the truth of Micaela's death for the first time—and curse myself for leaving my cell phone at home.

It starts to sprinkle. When I walk over to the railing and look down, I see a fellow on Platform Six, and I yell down to him and ask if he knows what's going on, but he just shrugs his shoulders. I then begin shouting in an attempt to rouse Ol' Man McNergal, the groundskeeper, knowing all the while it's pointless, since I've learned in my years of coming here that he naps deeply all afternoon.

Now it starts to rain in earnest, and since there's no cover I wander back over to Micaela's grave. "What kind of an imbecile designs a rotating graveyard?" I mutter. Soon I'm thoroughly drenched, the cold wind whipping right through me as I stand there shivering in the rain like an idiot.

"I'm sorry, Micaela!" I blurt out, noticing for the first time that, despite laboring for decades under the self-generated delusion that my sister was stillborn, her headstone bears *two* dates. Imagining that I had killed her in utero, an outcome that was no less tragic than the

reality, had acquitted me of direct agency but nevertheless failed to entirely assuage my guilt.

"I'm sorry, Micaela," I repeat more softly, tears min-
gling with the rain. "I swear I didn't mean to kill you.
I just wanted to frighten you, to push you away so I
could have a little space to myself. Was that too much
to ask? To be able to think or feel something that you
weren't aware of. To be able to keep a goddamn secret
from you. But you needed to know everything, as if we
were one person with two bodies. *That's* what I was
trying to show you, dangling your body from the top
of the Ferris wheel, that we were *two* people. That we
were separate."

The platform lurches forward, and I feel enormous
relief that I won't have to spend the night in the graveyard. But five seconds later it stops again, and as the
darkness descends I feel the profound weight of loneliness and despair, and I wonder what, if anything, I have
left to live for. I briefly entertain the notion of leaping
off the railing, but I haven't got the nerve, so I lie down
in the puddle at my feet and curl my body around my
sister's tombstone, clutching the cold marble and imagining that I am hugging Micaela in the flesh.

I sleep fitfully through a continuous downpour,
shivering continuously and awakened by thunder and
lightning when not by nightmares. In my final dream,
as the rain lets up and the dawn finally arrives, I am

floating down a river in an open casket, vultures circling overhead and natives on the riverbank issuing war cries and flinging crude spears toward me. One of them arcs true and pierces my heart. I float down the river with the spear sticking straight up, slowly dying and barely conscious, and just as the vultures swoop down and begin pecking at my eyes, I awaken.

It's almost noon by the time they fix the machinery and the cemetery resumes its inane rotation. Though the sun has dried out my clothes, as I step off Platform Seven and head toward the bus stop, I still feel chilled to the bone, am achy from having shivered all night long, and sense a cold coming on. And as I approach the place where I bought the Ink, I realize I would like nothing better than to escape—for any length of time— from my wretched reality, so I enter the alley, wondering if I might be able to score another hit.

Aside from a couple of scrawny cats, the alley is vacant, leaving me bereft of hope. But as I turn around and head back to the street I notice some stairs leading down to a doorway, above which is a small hand-lettered sign that reads META.

I walk down the stairs and knock on the heavy metal door. No one answers. I notice a buzzer and press it, and a muffled voice emerges from a small speaker asking me for the password. I think for a moment and say, "Incognolio," and the door clicks open.

CHAPTER ELEVEN

WORDS ON A PAGE

Muldoon sneezes as he walks through the door, his face a portrait of dejection, and I can't help feeling bad for heaping such misery upon him. Then again, a contented protagonist doesn't make for much of a story. Perhaps if he didn't take it all so seriously it might take the edge off, or so I thought when I first envisioned our metaleptic rendezvous.

"You look like you could use a drink," I tell him, offering the stool next to mine at the bar. "Hey, Smirnoff. How about a Jack Daniels on the rocks for the gentleman?"

The bartender pours the whiskey and I have him add it to my tab.

"How'd you know my drink?" Muldoon asks, and then gulps down half the pour.

"I can read you like a book, Muldoon." I smile and sip my daiquiri, figuring that the lighting in Meta is too dim for him to recognize me.

"Huh. What are you, psychic or something?"

"Not exactly."

"Didn't catch your name." Muldoon offers his hand. "Micaela," I reply, and we briefly make contact. "You met a version of me once before, when you were tripping on Ink."

"*Micaela?*" He squints at me. "What the hell are *you* doing here? I thought you only existed in an alternate universe."

I pause, wondering how to best frame our discussion.

Muldoon glances around the room. "What is this place, anyway? Why did I need a password to get in?"

"It's exclusive."

"I can see that. Aside from the bartender, we're the only ones here."

"Yes, I wanted privacy," I say. "I need to tell you something important."

Muldoon sneezes. I offer him a tissue and he blows his nose.

"Another round," I tell Smirnoff, thinking this might be easier if Muldoon's had a couple.

He knocks back the second whiskey and says, "Shoot."

"You see, I'm writing a novel," I say. "And you're in it."

"Okay." Muldoon runs his hand through his hair. "So, do you want feedback? I'd be happy to look at the manuscript."

"That's kind of you," I say. "But here's the thing. *This* is the manuscript."

Muldoon frowns. "What do you mean?"

"I'm writing our dialogue as we speak." I look for a glimmer of realization in his eyes, but he just stares at me blankly. "This is the scene in my novel, Muldoon, where I inform you that you're the protagonist in the story I'm writing."

"Okaaay." Muldoon signals Smirnoff for another drink and downs it. "Are you telling me that I'm not real?"

"It's more complicated than that. You see, I had a twin brother who was stillborn. I named him Muldoon, and in my novel, I imagine what might have happened if *I'd* died and he'd survived."

Muldoon pinches the bridge of his nose.

"So, none of this is real." He throws his glass to the floor and it shatters. "That glass didn't just break?"

"Sure, it broke in the story," I say. "But there are no real-world consequences. That's what I'm trying to impress upon you, Muldoon. Don't take everything so seriously. Ultimately, it's just words on a page."

Muldoon falls silent. His expression is sullen.

"Then *you're* not real either," he points out. "You're just another character in the story."

"That's correct. I'm a fictional version of myself. In actuality, I'm sitting at my desk and typing this dialogue."

"Guess I'll have to take your word for it," says Muldoon. "What's the name of your novel?"

"*Incognolio*. Same as yours."

"And what the hell *is* Incognolio?"

"Damned if I know. The word just came to me."

"Well, I'm fed up with the whole stinking business." Muldoon gets up to leave. "And I want nothing further to do with you or your goddamn novel."

"Wait, Muldoon, don't leave." I grab his wrist. "I thought this information would *help* you."

"Help me?" He snickers. "How so?"

"I don't know. Give you some distance. Provide a broader perspective as things continue to unravel."

Muldoon wrenches his wrist free from my grasp. "Why don't you just leave me the fuck alone?" He turns and walks out the door, slamming it behind him.

At first I feel bad, wishing I had handled the situation better. But then I recall that conflict is what drives a good story, so perhaps it's just as well. Anyhow, I'll have to worry about it later because I can hear my husband pulling into the driveway, so I save the file and quickly close the laptop. I grab a book and settle onto the sofa just as Jack walks through the door.

Jack tosses his keys into a bowl and kicks off his shoes. He comes over and sits on the couch by my feet, but I don't look up from my book.

"Whatcha reading?" he asks.

"*Cosmicomics*," I mutter.

"Lame title. What's it about?"

"It's complicated." I wish he would leave me alone.

Jack snatches the book and throws it to the floor.

"You weren't even reading, were you?"

I say nothing.

"*Were* you?" he says louder. He slaps my face, and my body goes tingly-numb. "Admit it! You were on the damn computer again."

"I was just checking email."

"Yeah, and working on that story? I know you're writing about me."

I pout, looking up at Jack with my submissive sad-girl expression, and he calms down.

"I'm sorry, baby." He caresses the cheek that he slapped. "But you hafta promise me that you'll stop writing that crap, or I swear I'll throw out the damn laptop."

I tell Jack what he wants to hear and then he slides next to me on the sofa, strokes my hair and kisses my neck. I tolerate it until he puts his hand up my blouse and fondles my breasts.

"Not now, Jack. I'm not in the mood."

"I don't give a shit." He unsnaps my jeans and pulls them down to the ankles, along with my underwear. "*Get* in the bloody mood!"

I push him off of me and manage to get away, but with my pants still bunched at the ankles, I trip and fall to the carpet.

"Not this time." Jack pounces on me, rips my pants away, and rolls me over. "I have my goddamn rights."

"Bullshit!" I spit at his face and he slugs me in the eye.

Temporarily stunned, I just lie there. When he's done, Jack rolls off me, gets up, and walks to the kitchen. I hear him crack open a beer, and then open the sliding door leading out to the deck.

I stand up, feeling sore and disgusted, and go take a hot shower. I quickly get dressed, grab my purse, and head out the door. Soon I'm driving down the freeway, in a daze, when I realize that I'm late for my writers' group, so I get off at the next exit, backtrack, and head to Paula's house.

"Jesus," says Paula when she sees my shiner. She gives me a long hug.

I walk into her dining room, where Piper and Paige are sitting at the table, thumbing through their copies of the *Incognolio* chapters I'd emailed to them.

"Oh no, not again," says Piper when she gets a look at my battered face. "You poor thing."

"When are you gonna leave the fucker once and for all?" asks Paige. "Come stay with me, Micaela."

Standing there, surrounded by such love and concern, tears well up in my eyes. But then I feel dizzy and sick to my stomach, and I fall to the floor.

CHAPTER TWELVE

BLACK SNAKE WHIP

When I come to, I'm lying on the living room floor, surrounded by Paula, Piper, and Paige.

"Here, drink some water," Paula says. "How are you feeling?"

"Better."

We get up and all sit around the table. Paula hands me a bag of frozen peas, which I press against my eye. Then she pours me some Sauvignon Blanc and tops off the other glasses.

"I'm really impressed with your writing, Micaela," says Paige. "You've come a long way."

"Absolutely," Paula says. "And your male narrator is really authentic. Writing from the point of view of the opposite gender isn't easy to pull off."

"True," Piper says. "If anything, Muldoon is more believable than Arielle or Delphia. I found them a bit stereotypical."

"I'm portraying them as Muldoon would write them," I say. "They're basically male-fantasy women."

"Okay," Piper replies. "That makes sense."

"Some of the names are a hoot," Paula says. "How did you come up with Yiddle?"

"When I was a kid I had a parakeet named Yiddle."

"How about the twin?" asks Piper. "Did you really have a stillborn twin?"

I nod. "I've been obsessed with him my entire life. The guilt I'm left with probably explains why I've always been attracted to abusive men." It may be delusional, and I'd never admit it aloud, but a part of me hopes that finishing *Incognolio* will finally heal me so I can be done once and for all with men like Jack.

"Wow," Paula says. "But you don't actually blame yourself for it, do you?"

"Not consciously, of course. But on some level I think I'm convinced I killed him." I sip some wine. "But this isn't group therapy, guys. What about my writing?"

"I think it's really creative," Piper says. "But if you want to get published, you might want to make it a little less...quirky."

"I know you hate outlining, Micaela," says Paula. "But it could help organize the story and keep it on track."

"But I don't *want* it on track." I hear the defensiveness in my voice. "The whole idea is to let my imagination run amuck.'

"Exactly," Paige says. "That's what I love about it. You can't predict what'll happen next."

"I don't know," Piper says. "Parts of it are pretty out there. I'm afraid editors might be put off by that near-incest scene. It's sort of icky."

"Fuck editors," I say. "I'm writing this one for myself. If I don't get it published, so be it."

"There's always self-publishing," Paula offers.

"Hold on," Paige says. "I thought the purpose of this group was to help each other write the best novel we're capable of producing."

Everyone agrees, so we return to discussing the technical and artistic merits of the manuscript. When the meeting is over, Paige reiterates her invitation for me to stay at her place. I make excuses, but she insists. So I thank her and then drive home to pick up some clothes and my laptop.

Jack is hammered by now and becomes agitated when I inform him of my plans.

"You're not staying with that dyke." He stands in the bedroom doorway, holding a bottle of Corona, watching me pack. "She's just trying to get in your pants."

"I'm not discussing it."

I shut my suitcase, squeeze past him, and am nearly out the front door when I feel a tremendous blow to my skull and black out.

When I awaken, I find myself naked and spread eagled on the bed, wrists and ankles shackled to the bedposts. My head throbs with pain.

"Sorry, baby," Jack says, "but this is for your own good."

"Yeah? How so?"

"Only pain can relieve your crushing guilt." Jack grins. "You know, from killing your brother?"

"Fuck you," I say, cursing the day I told him about Muldoon.

Jack says he'll be right back and returns a minute later with a fresh beer and a black snake whip. I didn't realize he owned any sort of whip, and the sight of it elicits a strange sensation, like an electrical current streaking from my heels to the crown of my head.

"Quit it, Jack. I'll have you arrested, I swear."

"Not likely, babe. I cut the phone line and I'm afraid you won't be leaving the house much anymore."

My breath grows shallow and irregular as Jack slowly draws the length of the whip through the fingers of his left hand, caressing the leather, and then lifts his arm and holds it in mid-air, enjoying the look of fear on my face.

A flick of his wrist and my belly is on fire, but I force myself to remain silent. He whips my hips, my thighs, my shins, my feet, and then my breasts, whooping like a moron when he lands one on a nipple. Each snap of the whip produces a thunderous cracking sound, along with a searing pain that travels up my body and gathers at the base of my skull. Jack increases the tempo and viciousness of the blows, flailing away like a maniac. Soon my entire body is covered with bright red lash marks, the agony unbearable, but I refuse him the satisfaction of hearing me cry.

Finally, Jack drops the whip and then his drawers. He stands above me, stroking his enormous boner.

"You sick fuck," I manage to say despite my shaking voice and labored breathing.

"Oh, the fun has just begun," he says. "I've been waiting for this for a long time."

Jack finishes his beer, tosses the bottle aside, and then leaps on the bed, looming over me as he positions himself between my legs.

"Hope you're in the mood," he says, winking.

My entire body pulsating in pain, I close my eyes and am bracing myself for penetration when I hear a

loud *thwack* and then a dull thud, as something heavy
falls to the floor.

"Good thing I keep this in my trunk," says Paige, and
when I open my eyes she's brandishing a tire iron.

Jack lies in a heap on the carpet, the side of his head
a bloody mess. Paige feels for a pulse, then takes a couple of neckties from Jack's closet and secures his wrists
and ankles.

When she has released my restraints, I stand up
slowly, unsteady on my feet. Paige wraps me in an embrace and I convulse in her arms, pouring out all the
tears I'd held back.

When I'm all cried out, Paige takes my hand and
leads me to the bathroom, where she cleans the angry
red lash marks with soap and water, pats them dry, and
then sprays them with antiseptic.

It hurts like hell to get dressed, and when I'm done,
Jack comes to.

"Come on, babe." He struggles against his restraints.
"I was just fooling around."

I pick up the suitcase and stare down at him.

"You can't leave me like this."

"Don't worry, the police will untie you. Until then,
enjoy your blue balls."

Ignoring Jack's insults and promises of revenge, we
leave and drive down to the station.

"How did you know to come for me?" I ask Paige once she's parked the car.

"I know Jack," she says. "And it was taking you too damn long to pack a suitcase."

In the police station, I give a full report and a female cop takes photos of my wounds and the nasty lump on my head. Then Paige drives me to her house, a cute bungalow with a private beach. She carries my suitcase to her guest room, a cozy affair with a desk facing the ocean.

I spend two whole days flat on my back, recuperating, with little to do but think. Part of me feels bad for having Jack arrested, even though the bastard deserves it. It's tough to admit, but on some level I was aroused by the restraints and the whipping. The feeling of being utterly helpless and overpowered was…exciting.

I remember hearing a psychologist talking on the radio about her research on female sexuality, and how a large percentage of women fantasize about being raped. She cited one theory suggesting that rape was common in prehistoric times, so natural selection favored females who experienced some arousal from being overpowered, since the resulting vaginal lubrication would diminish the damage inflicted on their sexual organs. Who knows if it's true, but I prefer to believe that rationale rather than consider myself a masochist.

I'm grateful to have a friend like Paige. After two days of lying in bed while she attends to my wounds, brings me food, and reads to me, I'm feeling restless, so I pull out my laptop and get back to work on the novel.

CHAPTER THIRTEEN

BREAK OUT
OF OUR CAGES!

I wake up hung over from the three whiskies I had at
META, plus several more that I drank when I got home,
but my muscles no longer ache and the cold I had yesterday appears to have miraculously disappeared. As I
brew myself some Krakatoan dark roast, I realize that
the reason I've felt so alienated from myself is that I'm
not writing this manuscript after all. *Micaela* is, and
she's putting these words in my mouth.

Sitting in my breakfast nook, sipping coffee and
gazing out the window, I feel exposed and violated, all
sense of privacy demolished. My life, my very thoughts,
an open book.

An *actual* book. Words on a fucking page. I'm a fictitious character dreamed up by my twin sister, who has
nothing better to do than fantasize about what might

have happened if she'd died instead of me, and to turn those fantasies into a story of misery and despair.

I have to wonder why Micaela went out of her way to inform me that I'm not real, just a pathetic mario-nette in her control, with no free will, no autonomy, absolutely nothing to call my own. Not even these mo-rose thoughts, which she devises herself and attributes to me.

Why couldn't she have left me blissfully ignorant as I blunder my way through the malevolent maze of her twisted tale? Making a total mess of things, but at least possessing some sense of purpose. The conviction that, if I applied myself—used my intuition and intelligence, such as it is—I might solve the mystery of Incognolio and in the process free myself.

All that is gone now, all sense of urgency and moti-vation, leaving in their wake a withered husk, the mere shadow of a man, a pitiful puppet who knows he's nothing but cloth and buttons.

What is there to do but off myself? But I know that if I try, I will somehow manage to survive—miracle of miracles—since protagonists cannot be knocked off partway through a novel.

I finish my coffee and then check to see how Yiddle is doing. Not only does she still look depressed, she's begun to pluck out her own feathers, some of which are scattered on the bottom of the cage, small bare patches now visible on her breast.

I pick up the box of parrot pellets, but then see that she hasn't touched the pellets or the fruits and veggies I gave her yesterday.

"What's the matter, girl?" I ask. "Should I take you to the vet?"

No vet. No vet, she weakly squawks.

"Why are you so unhappy?"

Existential angst, she replies, surprising me with her vocabulary.

"How come? What's bothering you?"

No meaning, quoth the parrot, and she plucks out yet another gray feather.

"You're telling me, pal." I look at her and sigh. "Well, for starters, we can free you from this damn cage."

I unlatch the cage door and Yiddle pokes her head out, blinks a few times, and then flies through the air, circling the room, already beginning to look more chipper.

"That's the ticket, Yiddle," I say. "Break out of our cages! If there's no free will, then we can do whatever the fuck we want."

A moment's thought reveals the illogical nature of my previous statement, but at this point I have no interest whatsoever in remaining rational.

"Hell, let's go for a stroll," I say, and Yiddle swoops in and perches on my left shoulder.

I walk downstairs and head west on Random Road, enjoying the fresh air and the briny scent wafting in from the sea. Ko drives by in his Lamborghini convertible and we smile and wave to each other. That's another cage I've broken out of: I no longer have to worry about keeping track of my subplots, or even differentiating fiction from so-called real life.

Soon I reach Circle Square and out of habit stop in at Hrabal's Tavern. Hrabal greets me and I take a stool at the bar.

His usual, squawks Yiddle.

"And your finest water for my feathered friend."

"Ah, an African Grey." Hrabal pours me a Jack Daniels and sets out a bowl of water. "Smartest bird on the planet, they say."

Smarter than they, notes Yiddle.

"Scores low on humility," I whisper to Hrabal.

The door opens and in walks Delphia, looking scrumptious in a burgundy blouse, black mini, black patterned stockings, and pumps.

Ay, caramba! squawks Yiddle.

"Welcome, my sweet." I pull out a stool for her and kiss her on both cheeks.

"A dry martini for the lady," I say. "A lady, please note, who always knows just when to enter a scene."

Delphia smiles demurely, and then looks me over.

"How are you holding up, Muldoon?"

"What do you mean?"

"I have the Faloosh," she reminds me. "It showed me what happened."

"Oh, that."

Delphia raises an eyebrow and waits.

"Okay, I admit it was traumatic," I say. "Shit, it's not every day that you find out you're fictional."

Words on a fucking page! squawks Yiddle.

"You'll get used to it," Delphia says.

"But how do I come to terms with having no free will? Knowing that everything I say or do is set in ink?"

"You're forgetting one crucial point." Delphia downs her martini and signals Hrabal for another round. "What a novelist writes is driven by her unconscious, so her characters take on lives of their own."

I sip my whiskey and mull this over.

"So, you're saying that Micaela doesn't control us?"

"Not consciously," Delphia says. "It's like a waking dream. And there's another advantage."

"What's that?"

"Once the book is published, you're immortal."

I have mixed feelings about the prospect of immortality, so I choose to gloss over that point and instead say, "What do we do next? Solve the mystery of the epidemic?"

"That can wait." Delphia reaches out and gently strokes my inner thigh. "How would you like to explore my…Incognolio?"

Innuendo! *Innuendo*! squawks Yiddle.

So, I head on home with Yiddle on my shoulder and my arm around Delphia. Soon we're in bed and I'm stripping off her stockings, kissing her legs and perfect feet, kissing her breasts and luscious mouth, having glorious sex for the first time in ages…or for the first time ever, if Micaela is to be believed.

When we're done and I'm lying there exhausted, the phone rings. I let it go to message.

"Hey, dickwad," says the grating voice of Dick Fracken. "How's the manuscript coming along? You have exactly one week to deliver the completed draft, or expect another visit from Grunt."

CHAPTER FOURTEEN

TWELVE-INCH PIANIST

It's pure joy waking up with Delphia in my arms after having spent the entire afternoon and evening making love, hearing now her soft breathing as she sleeps, inhaling her scent of honeysuckle and warm bread, gazing at her serene, adorable face.

I suppose it's not surprising that I find her so attractive, given that she's my creation. But then I remember that I'm not writing the book. At least Micaela got one thing right.

I carefully disentangle myself from Delphia and tiptoe out of the bedroom, make some coffee, and then place a call to Fracken.

"You're interrupting my massage, asshole," he barks.

"Just returning your call."

"Well, how many pages have you finished? What's your word count?"

"Here's the thing," I say. "Turns out I'm not writing the manuscript. My twin sister is."

"What the fuck are you talking about, Muldoon?"

"This will sound strange, but you and I are actually characters in the novel she's writing."

"If you're trying to weasel your way out of ghost-writing *Incognolio*, you'd better come up with a better excuse than that."

"But it's true."

"Because your goddamn sister said so?"

"Well, it wasn't exactly my sister," I say. "Just a fictional representation of her."

"Do you think I'm an idiot, Muldoon?" In a muted voice, he continues, "Forget the rest. Skip to the happy ending," and I'm about to object that I don't know how *Incognolio* ends, and that furthermore you can't just skip writing the middle of a book, but then his voice comes back, loud and clear, "You have one damn week to finish the thing. Miss the deadline and you're dead meat."

Fracken hangs up and I heave a sigh, distressed at the prospect of having to deal with another visit from Grunt.

But my mood lightens when Delphia appears in the doorway, wearing my bathrobe. I kiss her, pour her a cup of coffee, and fry up some eggs.

While eating breakfast, I think back on my conversation with Fracken.

"Something's bugging me," I tell Delphia. "Why should we assume that Micaela was telling the truth?"

"What do you mean?"

"Maybe she fabricated the whole thing." I finish my eggs and wipe my mouth. "Hell, she offered no proof. How do we know for sure that somewhere out there is a real-life Micaela typing what I'm saying?"

"I guess we don't," Delphia says. "But how can we possibly find out?"

"Let's get dressed. I've got an idea."

Soon the two of us are heading west on the #33 bus, and I pull the cord as we approach my usual stop.

"Are we visiting Micaela's grave?" Delphia asks.

"Nope. We're going to META."

Delphia and I enter the desolate alleyway and walk down the concrete stairs to the club. I ring the buzzer, and the same muffled voice asks me for the password.

"Incognolio," I say with confidence.

"Sorry, no entrance," replies the voice.

"Huh, must've changed it," I tell Delphia. "What else could it be?"

I try several alternatives without success, and then hear a voice from above.

"Just screwing with you guys," says Micaela, looking down at us from the top of the stairs.

"Very funny." Delphia and I climb the stairs. "Delphia, this is my sister, Micaela. Micaela—well, I suppose there's no need to introduce you to your own character."

The two women shake hands, sizing each other up.

"I've been expecting you," Micaela says.

"Naturally," I say. "Because you're directing the whole shebang, right?"

Micaela smiles.

"Well, then undoubtedly you're aware that we've come to see some kind of proof of what you claim."

"Entirely reasonable," Micaela says. "What would you like to see?"

I glance up and down the alley and recall my first encounter there.

"Let's start small." I put out my palm. "Make some Ink appear."

In a flash, a dozen or so tablets—black with a gold spot in the middle—materialize in my hand. I exchange looks with Delphia, then thrust the pills in my pocket for safekeeping.

"Could've been slight-of-hand," says Delphia, and I nod in agreement.

"Okay, let's see you change the weather," I say, and it immediately starts snowing. Purple snow, at that.

I catch a flake in my hand and watch it melt into a drop of purple water in my palm.

"Impressive," Delphia says. "But the flake could be a fluke."

At this point I'm convinced it's not a fluke, but I'm sensing an opportunity here, a way to turn this little game to my advantage. "That's right. We need something conclusive." Then it comes to me, and I wonder why it took so long. "Give me a twelve-inch penis. And that's P-E-N-I-S, not P-I-A-N-I-S-T."

My jeans become awfully tight in the crotch. I pull out the waistband and glance down, then over at Delphia. She leans over to take a look and her eyes bulge out.

"Mamma mia," she says.

"Something tells me you're sleeping over tonight," I say.

"Doesn't take the Faloosh to figure that one out," Delphia says.

Muldoon and Delphia are giggling like idiots when I hear Paige scream, "Holy shit! A tidal wave!"

I look up from my laptop and sure enough, there's a twenty-foot wall of water surging toward the bungalow.

CHAPTER FIFTEEN

DEMONS AND GOBLINS AND GRIFFINS, OH MY!

Paige has prepared a delicious Cobb salad for lunch, and the two of us are enjoying it out on her back deck, facing the placid sea.

"How's the story coming along?" she asks.

"Super," I say. "Nothing inspires writing better than a magnificent view of the ocean."

"Yeah, I love it here."

I sip the Chardonnay and then fill my lungs with the salty air.

"I almost destroyed this place with a tidal wave, but I couldn't do it. I like staying here."

"Were you going to drown me?"

"I was considering it, but I feel our relationship has potential." I smile coyly. "Think about it. Two female novelists living together. Rivalry. Underlying sexual tension."

"Great stuff," Paige says. "I just wish *I* could get going on an idea. I've been blocked for months."

"You should go see my therapist, Baraka. She's helped me through several periods of drought."

"*Could* I? You wouldn't mind sharing her?"

"Not at all. She has excellent boundaries, so it shouldn't be a problem."

After lunch, I try to resume writing outside on the deck, but I'm not in the mood, so I go for a barefoot walk on the beach. I wish I could take a swim, but know that the salt water would sting my still-healing lash wounds.

I'm finished with Jack, that's for sure. Baraka had warned me not to marry him, but I didn't listen. Pathologically attracted to angry men, I'm always convinced that my love can heal them. Instead, their anger inevitably turns on me, which I feel I deserve for having failed to induce transformation.

I've learned in therapy that much of this stems from my childhood attempts to rescue my father, a morose man with an explosive temper, whose bitterness was only exacerbated when my brother was born dead. Mostly he blamed my mother, who refused to stop drinking during pregnancy, but I always sensed that he blamed me as well, and secretly wished that his son had survived and not me.

As an only child with no pets or companions, it's not surprising that I invented an imaginary friend. I named my vanished brother Muldoon, and the two of us became inseparable. Muldoon was mischievous and made me laugh, and he never betrayed me or disclosed the many secrets I shared with him.

My parents grudgingly put up with Muldoon, hoping I'd tire of him as I aged. But I didn't, and by the time I was eight, they insisted on taking me to a shrink. Dr. Schmendrik told me that I blamed myself for my brother's death, and insisted that only by giving up Muldoon could I properly mourn the loss and start making real friends. He helped me conduct a funeral service for Muldoon in the backyard of the clinic, complete with a miniature coffin he'd built himself. It was that night that I started cutting myself.

A mechanical beeping sound disrupts my morbid reverie. Looking to my left, I see a cute little girl jumping up and down with a metal detector in her hands.

"I found something!" she cries.

Her enthusiasm infects me, instantly eradicating the last traces of moroseness. "Cool!" I say. "Want some help?"

The girl nods, and we both start digging in the sand. She tells me her name is Scout and she's eight years old.

"Have you ever discovered anything before?"

"Sure, tons of stuff. Yesterday I found a tuna fish can, two quarters, and a belt buckle. Last week I found a jackknife, but my dad wouldn't let me keep it." I dig for several minutes, and I'm beginning to think we're in the wrong spot when Scout yells out, "Look! What's this?"

"I'm not sure." I clear away more sand. "Some sort of box."

It's quite heavy, constructed from an unusual metal that's blacker than black. Once Scout and I have cleared away enough sand, it takes both of us to lift the box out of the hole we've dug.

"Quick, open it!" Scout says.

Peels of thunder rumble in the distance. A baritone voice bellows from the heavens: "It is *forbidden* to open the box!"

"Who the hell was that?" I say, glancing around.

Scout looks up at me with eyes full of rebellion. "Nobody tells me what to do," she says. "Come on, it's probably buried treasure!"

"Are you sure?"

Scout vigorously nods her head, and it seems that her rebelliousness is contagious too, as I'm suddenly eager to know what's in the box.

"Well, there's a combination lock. We need a ten-letter word."

Scout tries out several words, manipulating a row of ten dials, each dial containing the entire alphabet. She dials *barefooted, watermelon,* and *everything,* but none of them work. She tries *randomness, butterflies,* and *bamboozled,* without success.

"We'll never get it," Scout whimpers, as the thunder crackles. "There are too many words."

"Try *Incognolio,*" I say, spelling it out for her. Scout dials the word and the lid of the box pops open.

"Hooray!" Scout cries. "How'd you know?"

"Just a hunch."

The two of us gaze into the box and Scout groans.

"It's empty!"

"That's odd," I say. "Why bury a box with an elaborate lock, forbid anyone to open it, and put nothing inside?"

As we stare into the box, the blackness within it seems to grow darker. A clash of cacophonous sounds blasts forth, nearly deafening us, and then all manner of dreadful beasts—demons and goblins and gorgons and griffins, dragons and hellhounds and hydras and harpies—all burst out of the box, whirl in a giant circle over our heads, and then fly off in every direction.

Overhead, gray clouds swirl with furious energy, and as the thunder booms, a form takes shape. The fierce visage of an older man appears, with flowing gray locks, angry eyes, and a full white beard.

Scout clasps my hand, giving me strength.

"How dare you!" Zeus growls. "Just like Pandora, you have defied me. Yet more evils are unleashed upon this Earth!"

"Um…sorry about that?" says Scout, smiling.

"Your remorse is of no use!" Zeus roars. "You have sealed humanity's doom."

And as quickly as the face formed, it scatters and is gone. Rain begins to fall.

"Big grouch." Scout slams the lid of the box closed. "What a meanie!"

"Don't worry about him." I put my arm around Scout and hug her to my side. "Why don't we get you home?"

Scout goes shifty-eyed and then pulls at a wet earlobe.

"You do have a home, don't you? You mentioned your dad."

"That was kind of a fib." Scout stands up as the rain washes over her. "My parents died in a plane crash last year. My stupid foster parents beat me, so I ran away."

"And you're living on the beach?" I maneuver the box back into the pit and cover it with the sand we'd dug up.

Scout nods, so I tell her she can stay with me and Paige, and the two of us are running back to the bungalow, lightning striking the ground and the roiling sea, when I experience a sharp stinging pain on the back of my neck and cry out.

Paige comes out onto the deck, where I sit at my laptop. "Sorry, Micaela. I forgot to warn you about the bees. Come on, I've got some benzocaine swabs in the bathroom."

CHAPTER SIXTEEN

WOMB TWIN SURVIVORS

"Over two thousand years ago, the Greek philosopher Plato proposed that people are conceived perfect, and then split in half by Zeus. These split-aparts are forever searching for one another in order to join together and regain their original sense of wholeness."

That's how Dr. Cassandra Didymos opens the meeting of the local support group for Womb Twin Survivors. There are seven of us sitting in a circle along with the doctor, a self-proclaimed expert on the syndrome. Chagrined by my failure to make progress on the novel over the last few days, I have come in search of an alternative source of healing, inspiration, or both.

"This ancient myth is typically applied to the concept of soul mates, but it also resonates with those of us who lost a twin sibling in the womb. Even if the child is never made aware that a twin has vanished, a survivor often feels that part of the self is missing, and may suffer from a profound sense of melancholy, loneliness, worthlessness, and longing. Underlying feelings of guilt and shame can result in obsessions, compulsions, eating disorders, self-destructive behaviors, difficulty forming intimate or lasting bonds, and a propensity for developing codependent relationships.

"Some have questioned or ridiculed the idea of fetal memory, but we have found that under hypnosis many survivors can reconnect with the emotions and bodily sensations they experienced in the womb. Hearing the stories of other survivors can also rekindle memories. It is through remembering, feeling, and forgiving that real healing can take place."

"But before we begin, there are two newcomers to the group," she says, and introduces both me and Chester, a man in his thirties. "Why don't the two of you tell us a little about what brings you here tonight?"

Chester glances my way, and I ask him to go first.

"Well, my twin actually made it to term, so maybe I don't belong here." Chester looks over at Dr. Didymos, and she gestures for him to continue. "See, Rochester was my identical twin, and we looked so much alike that without clothes, no one could tell us apart.

"One day when we were six months old, my mama was giving us a bath when the phone rang. Folks say that by the time she returned to the bathroom, my brother had tipped over and drowned."

There are several gasps and the doctor says, "I'm so sorry."

"Well, it was bad enough losing a sibling," Chester says. "But my parents weren't sure which of us had died, so they flipped a coin and decided it was Rochester. Time passed, and as I grew older I began to wonder who actually drowned. Perhaps it was Chester who died and I was really Rochester."

"Does it matter?" asks the woman seated next to me.

"Damn straight, it matters!" Chester waves his arms. "I could be an imposter, and I've got no way of knowing for sure. So I started drinking. Became alcoholic. Sometimes I like to get plastered and take a swim during riptide, half-hoping I won't be able to make it back to shore."

The group goes silent for some time, and then Dr. Didymos thanks Chester and says, "His story illustrates the depth of the emotional bond and shared identity that can form between twins." Then she asks me to say a few words.

"My brother nearly made it to term," I say. "I'm told that he expired just days before the delivery. Under hypnosis, I recalled how close I felt to Muldoon, almost like we were a single being."

Several of the group members nod and then wait for me to continue, childlike expressions of wonder on their faces.

"They say that the late-term fetus can hear her mother's heartbeat," I say. "Well, for me, my mother's heartbeat was muffled and distant-sounding. But Muldoon's heartbeat was my constant companion, more comforting than the thumb in my mouth. When it stopped, a part of me died."

One group member begins to weep softly, and the doctor passes a box of tissues around the circle.

"Again, this was under hypnosis, so I can't be certain it's accurate," I continue. "But what I recovered was that I had somehow gotten my umbilical cord tangled up with my twin. I believe it was around his neck. Muldoon's heartbeat started racing. I remember struggling, wanting to help him, but I couldn't. My brother's heartbeat, the one sound that calmed and consoled me, fell silent."

After another pregnant pause, Dr. Didymos asks me how this early history has affected my life.

"I'd like to be counted among the worried well, or even the walking wounded, Doc. But the truth is, I'm one of the crawling crippled. I dropped out of high school and have never been able to hold onto a job. I was anorexic for years and used to cut myself just to feel anything at all. I've been sexually promiscuous since my early teens, and I always end up with guys who beat and mistreat me. I've had mono and anemia and major depression and chronic fatigue syndrome and just about every other damn disease that leaves you feeling half-dead. Underneath it all, I feel empty and incomplete. Not to mention the crushing guilt of knowing that, before I even drew my first breath, I destroyed the most precious thing in the world."

By this point the whole group is in tears, and I'm wondering whether it was a mistake to come. The doctor asks if there's anything that makes me feel better.

"Writing," I reply. "I'm working on a novel in which I died and Muldoon survived. But even that's begun to sour. Today I shifted the story away from my brother, because it's just too painful."

"You must stick with this pain," says Dr. Didymos. "This pain is what can save you."

My ribcage contracts, making it difficult to breathe. "But I'm afraid that Muldoon will die and I'll have to lose him all over again."

"Yes." The doctor sighs. "I know."

By the time the meeting ends I'm emotionally drained, but at the same time I'm inspired because Dr. Didymos's promptings have given me renewed hope that I can find healing through my novel. Perhaps my desire to keep my brother safe is the reason I'm stuck, and what I really need to do is accept the possibility of having to let him go.

As soon as I get back to the bungalow, even though it's late at night, I sit down at my laptop and return to the world of Muldoon.

CHAPTER SEVENTEEN

ONTOLOGY OF FICTION

Delphia and I haven't left our little love nest in days. Hell, we've barely gotten out of bed except to hit the john or pay the take-out delivery guys, the two of us whooping it up with the 12-inch penis like little kids with a fancy new toy.

Yiddle is living the good life, too—free of her cage, gorging on piles of parrot pellets and leftover take-out. I even had a mate delivered for her, a male African Grey we named Yazzle.

Hedonism rules! squawks Yiddle.

True, we have the inevitable visit from Grunt hanging over our heads, but that's still several days away, and we're bound to figure out something by then.

Meanwhile, my fabulous custom-made girlfriend and more-than-generous physical endowment have sent

my self-esteem through the roof, and my old feelings of
guilt have vanished, now that I realize the Ferris wheel
incident in which I killed Micaela was purely fictional.

All of which makes me a pretty lousy protagonist
at this point—largely devoid of inner conflict, external
goals, or significant obstacles. But it may not take much,
I fear, to topple my house of cards.

Yiddle flutters about, squawking, *Pizza! Pizza!*

I head downstairs, since Yiddle is rarely wrong, and
sure enough the pizza delivery guy is arriving at the
door.

I greet him and he says, "Here's your—whoa, dude.
You're hung like a linguini!"

"Thank you," I say. Under other circumstances I
would have put on some clothes for his comfort, but
since none of this is actually happening, then I'm not
really naked. "Come upstairs—I forgot my wallet."

Pizza Guy follows me into my apartment, which is
a holy wreck. I introduce him to Delphia, who lounges
on the sofa in a kimono, applying jungle-green polish to
her toenails.

"Pleased to meet you, ma'am." He manages to maneuver the pizza onto the coffee table, which—like the
carpet—is littered with empty pizza boxes and Chinese take-out cartons, as well as empty beer, wine, and
Champagne bottles. "You folks celebrating something?"

Delphia smiles and says, "You could say that."

"We're rejoicing in our ontological status as fictional beings," I say.

Words on a fucking page! squawks Yiddle.

"I see," says Pizza Guy. "So, you support Peter van Inwagen's argument for the existence of *creatures of fiction?*"

"Uh…absolutely!" I reply, not having the first clue what he's talking about, and offer Pizza Guy a chair and a slice of pizza before I plop down on the sofa next to Delphia. "All I know is that I *feel* real. I don't see any words or letters here. I see a *world* around me and I'm in it."

"Ah, but what if no one is reading the text? Do you still exist?"

Delphia asks, "Does the moon disappear when no one's looking at it?"

"In a sense, it does," says Pizza Guy, who informs us that he's a grad student in theoretical physics at Imaginary University. "Among physicists, the leading approach to quantum mechanics—the Copenhagen Interpretation—suggests that there is no manifest reality in the absence of observation."

"Then I'm as real as the fucking moon." I wipe tomato sauce from my mouth with the back of my hand. "Or anything else in the so-called actual universe."

The phone rings. When I answer it, a voice on the other end asks for Schlomo.

"Wrong number," I say. I'm about to end the call when something prompts me to ask the caller's name and place him on speaker phone.

"Minor," he says.

"Minor?"

"Yeah. Minor Character."

Intrigued, I ask him to tell me a bit about himself.

"Not much to tell, I'm afraid. I interrupt your conversation by dialing a wrong number."

"And that's it?" It doesn't seem possible. "What were you doing before you placed this call?"

"Nothing."

"And at the end of our conversation you simply vanish?"

"Apparently. Hence the name."

"Right," I say. "But there's gotta be more to you than that. I mean, why do you even exist?"

"Comic relief, I suppose."

Yiddle squawks, *Hey, that's* my *gig.*

"Well, describe the room you're in," I say.

"No room."

"No room? What about the phone you're holding?"

"No phone. I'm just a disembodied voice," he says matter-of-factly. "Now if you don't mind I'm going to hang up."

"Hang up? But you said—"

"I know…there's no phone. I was speaking meta-phorically."

Minor "hangs up" and so do I.

"Fascinating," says Pizza Guy. "Even lacking a body, Minor is as real as we are."

I scratch my head, perhaps to make sure it's still there.

"Of course, there are drawbacks to being creatures of fiction," adds Pizza Guy.

"Drawbacks?" I repeat.

"Sure. Everything you value could vanish in a flash."

"How so?" I don't think I like where this is headed.

"Well, take that humongous schlong you're so proud of." Pizza Guy reaches for another slice of pie. "What if the author feels that it's shallow for men to base their self-esteem on something as random and superficial as the size of one's penis, so she decides to shrink yours?"

I shrug nonchalantly, as if I'm way more mature than that, and then shriek when my penis does indeed shrivel down to its original size.

"Or take your girlfriend, Delphia," says Pizza Guy. "You probably think you love her, right?"

"Um…sure," I mumble, still stunned as I stare at my shrunken genitals.

"But what if the author senses that your affection for Delphia is primarily based on physical attraction and decides to test this notion by increasing her age by, let's say, thirty years?"

No sooner does Pizza Guy utter these words than Delphia changes before my eyes from a ravishing woman to a still handsome, but gray-haired elderly lady.

Delphia doesn't appear surprised, so perhaps the Faloosh enabled her to anticipate this development. I, on the other hand, am mortified. Delphia is a sweet gal, and intelligent to boot, but I simply can't envision myself making love to a 60-something-year-old woman.

Bright side, squawks Yazzle, *no more condoms*!

"Yeah, thanks pal," I say.

"So, as you see," says Pizza Guy, "if you're a character in a fabulist novel such as this, you have to be prepared for unexpected transformations."

"No shit." Feeling more modest now, I walk over to the closet and throw on my trench coat. "But how the hell did you predict the changes? Do you have the Faloosh?"

"Don't need it," says Pizza Guy. "I'm at one with Incognolio."

"And what, pray tell, is Incognolio?"

Pizza Guy pauses, then opens his mouth as if to speak, pauses again, and now the whole living-room scene becomes hazzzzzzzzzzzzzzzzzzzzzzzzzzzzzzzzzzz zzzzzzzzzzzzzzzzzzzzzzzzzzzzzzzzzzzzzzzzzzzzzzzzzz zzzzzzzzzzzzzzzzzzzzzzzzzzzzzzzzzzzzzzzzzzzzzzzzzz

ZZZZZZZZZZZZZZZZZZZZZZZZZZZZZZZZZZZZZZZZZZZZZZZZZZZZ
ZZZZZZZZZZZZZZZZZZZZZZZZZZZZZZZZZZZZZZZZZZZZZZZZZZZZ
ZZZZZZZZZZZZZZZZZZZZZZZZZZZZZZZZZZZZZZZZZZZZZZZZZZZZ
ZZZZZZZZZZZZZZZZZZZZZZZZZZZZZZZZZZZZZZZZZZZZZZZZZZZZ
ZZZZZZZZZZZZZZZZZZZZZZZZZZZZZZZZZZZZZZZZZZZZZZZZZZZZ
ZZZZZZZZZZZZZZZZZZZZZZZZZZZZZZZZZZZZZZZZZZZZZZZZZZZZ
ZZZZZZZZZZZZZZZZZZZZZZZZZZZZZZZZZZZZZZZZZZZZZZZZZZZZ
ZZZZZZZZZZZZZZZZZZZZZZZZZZZZZZZZZZZZZZZZZZZZZZZZZZZZ
ZZZZZZZZZZZZZZZZZZZZZZZZZZZZZZZZZZZZZZZZZZZZZZZZZZZZ
ZZZZZZZZZZZZZZZZZZZZZZZZZZZZZZZZZZZZZZZZZZZZZZZZZZZZ
ZZZZZZZZZZZZZZZZZZZZZZZZZZZZZZZZZZZZZZZZZZZZZZZZZZZZ
ZZZZZZZZZZZZZZZZZZZZZZZZZZZZZZZZZZZZZZZZZZZZZZZZZZZZ
ZZZZZZZZZZZZZZZZZZZZZZZZZZZZZZZZZZZZZZZZZZZZZZZZZZZZ
ZZZZZZZZZZZZZZZZZZZZZZZZZZZZZZZZZZZZZZZZZZZZZZZZZZZZ
ZZZZZZZZZZZZZZZZZZZZZZZZZZZZZZZZZZZZZZZZZZZZZZZZZZZZ
ZZZZZZZZZZZZZZZZZZZZZZZZZZZZZZZZZZZZZZZZZZZZZZZZZZZZ
ZZZZZZZZZZZZZZZZZZZZZZZZZZZZZZZZZZZZZZZZZZZZZZZZZZZZ
ZZZZZZZZZZZZZZZZZZZZZZZZZZZZZZZZZZZZZZZZZZZZZZZZZZZZ
ZZZZZZZZZZZZZZZZZZZZZZZZZZZZZZZZZZZZZZZZZZZZZZZZZZZZ
ZZZZZZZZZZZZZZZZZZZZZZZZZZZZZZZZZZZZZZZZZZZZZZZZZZZZ
ZZZZZZZZZZZZZZZZZZZZZZZZZZZZZZZZZZZZZZZZZZZZZZZZZZZZ
ZZZZZZZZZZZZZZZZZZZZZZZZZZZZZZZZZZZZZZZZZZZZZZZZZZZZ

CHAPTER EIGHTEEN

DILDORPHIANS

I wake up with the dawn and gradually come to realize that instead of lying in bed, I'm hunched over in my desk chair, the side of my face smooshed up against the keyboard, a bit of drool smeared across several of the keys.

I slowly get to my feet and then do some stretching exercises to loosen up the stiffness in my limbs and lower back.

I can remember returning home from the Womb Twin Survivor meeting and then working on a Muldoon chapter, but my recollection of what I wrote is vague and dreamlike. Curious as to whether the material is any good, I sit back down at the desk and read through Chapter Seventeen, chuckling at the bits with Pizza Guy and Minor Character and pleased with how my nose landed on the perfect key when I fell asleep.

Then, to my astonishment, I find that I've already started the next chapter—*this* one—in which I describe how I woke up and stretched, read through the previous chapter, and discover that I'm in the process of writing at this very moment.

This is a revelation—even while I am seemingly going about my everyday life, I'm actually still typing out the story on my laptop.

But how could this be?

The truth is that I have been misleading readers all along. I am not actually living at Paige's bungalow by the sea. The reality is much stranger. So strange, in fact, that I have not the smallest hope you will believe it.

One week ago, I dreamed that I'd been abducted by aliens and was being held captive on their spacecraft, which was orbiting the Earth. Only it turned out that it wasn't a dream.

These alien creatures, called Dildorphians, have journeyed from the far side of the Milky Way, in search of Incognolio. Technologically, they are far more advanced than humans. But however brilliant they may be intellectually, the Dildorphians lack imagination. This is where I come in.

The Dildorphians believe that the human unconscious holds the key to Incognolio, which they hope will fulfill their spiritual longings, for despite all their technical knowledge they feel empty inside. So they have abducted me, a novelist, a delver into the psyche. Unlike so many accounts of alien abduction that detail how various orifices are probed, the Dildorphians are only interested in probing my mind. Specifically, they wish to gain access to the depths of my subconscious mind, where Incognolio supposedly dwells.

To this end, they have placed me in a small enclosure with dim lighting, and confined me to a comfortable zero-gravity chair, employing some sort of force field to prevent me from escaping. I recline, naked, with my laptop floating in mid-air, right in front of me. When I type English words that form comprehensible sentences, the pleasure center in my brain is electrically stimulated. However, if twenty seconds lapse without a word being typed, my bare feet receive a mild shock. Every ten seconds thereafter, the shocks double in strength.

Because the vehicle's cloaking device is on the fritz, time is of the essence; the longer I take to complete my task, the greater the likelihood that earthlings will detect the spacecraft. Therefore, to avoid delays, I am fed intravenously and all waste products are removed by a process that I prefer not to describe.

Having discovered that sleep deprivation deepens my access to the unconscious, the Dildorphians limit me to two hours of sleep per day, just enough to keep me from becoming psychotic. Meanwhile, machines monitor my level of wakefulness, and administer injections of amphetamines and other stimulants as needed.

The aliens have treated me decently up to this point, but that could be simply because I presumably have what they want. Their silver faces have a somewhat sinister appearance, so I can't help wondering how the Dildorphians will react if I fail to deliver what they seek. All I can do, I figure, is to relax and let the writing flow, try not to censor anything, and allow the story to go where it wants.

Therapists are guides to the unconscious, so I decide to see whether I can get some assistance from Baraka, my therapist in the story. Let's say that I've been emailing Baraka each new chapter of *Incognolio* as I complete it, and discussion of the novel-in-progress has been dominating my therapy sessions.

"I'm finding it harder and harder to write about Muldoon," I tell her. "And when I do, it turns into farce."

"Yes, Micaela, you appear to be distancing yourself from the character." Baraka rocks gently in her rocking chair. Shadow, her black Lab, settles down at my feet and starts licking my ankle. "Why do you suppose that is?"

"I'm not sure." I pause, mulling it over, until a shock to the soles of my feet prompts me to resume writing. "Ever since Muldoon realized that he's a fictional character, I find it tough to empathize with him. I mean, what would that be like, discovering that you're just a figment of someone's imagination?"

"Disorienting, to say the least."

"Yes, and that's exactly how I feel: disoriented. I'm so confused as to which direction to take the manuscript that I end up paralyzed. And I'm terrified of developing writer's block."

"Terrified? How come? You've struggled through bouts of it in the past and come out the other end."

"I know, but I never felt this desperate, Baraka. It feels like if I don't finish this novel and get it just right, the consequences could be perilous."

"How so? After all, it's just a book."

I reach down to pet Shadow's head and she licks the back of my hand. I don't want to tell Baraka about the Dildorphians or she might have me committed. Instead, just as I'm jolted by another shock, I change the subject.

"I'm tired of torturing Muldoon," I say. "That's what you have to do in a novel: put your protagonist through hell. But if my brother had lived, I'd like to think that I would've treated him lovingly."

"Like in the scene when Muldoon enters the alternate universe?"

"I was wondering how long it would take you to bring that up," I say. "I assumed you were freaked out by it."

"Not at all. Were *you?*"

"Well, it's a little embarrassing to write about attempting to seduce one's brother."

"I don't view it as a matter of incest, Micaela."

I am aware that I'm blushing, and appreciate that Baraka's smile is sympathetic and not teasing.

"No, I view that scene as portraying your wish to reunite and merge with your split-off self."

"Explain, please."

"I believe that as a young child you split off from a deep and authentic part of yourself, and took on a false persona to gain your parents' love and acceptance. This enduring split is what drives your preoccupation with a missing twin, your search for a soul mate, as well as your longing for some sort of mystical union, represented by Incognolio."

"So how can I get back in touch with my split-off self?"

"Keep writing, my dear." Baraka smiles. "Keep writing as if your life depended upon it."

Little did she know that it very well might.

CHAPTER NINETEEN

THE HEIMLICH PROPHECIES

"I'm afraid you're losing control of the narrative, Micaela," says Piper, who is hosting the writers' group at her home tonight. "Abducted by Dildorphians? I mean, come on…"

The first half of the meeting focused on Paula's novel-in-progress, *The Heimlich Prophecies*, and now the discussion has shifted over to *Incognolio*. During the break, Piper brought out white wine and a large glass platter of raw oysters that are now nearly gone.

"I have to agree with Piper," says Paula. "Alien abduction is old hat. And why add science fiction to a plot that's already overstuffed?"

I sip my Pinot Grigio and remind myself that they're only trying to help.

"Your continuity at this point is awfully tenuous," Piper says. "Whatever happened to Scout and the black box? Not to mention all the Muldoon subplots? You pique our interest and then leave us hanging. It's all a big tease."

"That's what I find so intriguing about the manuscript," Paige says. "The story keeps forging ahead, defying logic, and refusing to conform to our expectations. Perhaps you just prefer conventional storytelling."

"I'm open to innovation," says Piper. "But you can't thwart the reader at every turn and expect her to keep reading."

"So stop reading," I say, crushing a napkin in my fist. "Better yet, I'll drop out of the group."

"Now, Micaela, don't get defensive." Paula reaches over and massages my shoulder. "Piper's entitled to her opinion. And you know I love your writing, but I'm also frustrated by certain aspects of the story."

My jaw muscles clench. "Such as?"

"Well, for starters, I wish you'd stuck with Muldoon's story. He's charming in a strange sort of way, and I was growing attached to him when you suddenly shift over to *your* life. Frankly, it's just not as entertaining as Muldoon's. And your new narrator sounds pretty much like the old one."

"Okay." I take a deep breath. She's hit a sore point: I'm useless when it comes to differentiating narrative voices. "What else?"

"Well, first Incognolio is a cult's mantra, then it's a weird epidemic and the name on a creepy headband. Fine. But then it's also a psychedelic drug, a password, the combination to a lock, and the spiritual quest of some alien race. For goodness sake, why not settle on a meaning and stick to it?"

"Because I don't *know* the meaning, damn it!" I press my skull with both hands, feeling like I could lose it at any second. "Look, that's the whole point, isn't it? Everyone's searching for something that's ultimately unknowable."

"How profound," Piper says.

"Cut it out, Piper." Paige runs her hand through her close-cropped hair. "I think it's a good thing that Micaela's story makes us uncomfortable. Her novel is *meant* to be disturbing. Readers all too often just want to be entertained, to lose themselves in the illusion of a make-believe world. *Incognolio* systematically shatters that illusion."

"To what end?" Paula asks. "Merely to upset the reader?"

"To philosophically explore ultimate questions." Paige glances at me, as if to make sure that I'm okay with her going to bat for me. I nod, urging her on, relieved that *someone* can explain what I've been attempting. "Worlds flicker in and out of existence in the story. Time and again, we buy into the reality of a scene, only to be rudely reminded that the whole thing is contrived—a fictional construct. Eventually we're forced to wonder whether *our* reality could be fictional as well."

Piper and Paula laugh nervously.

"I'm pretty confident that we're flesh and blood." Piper points to the bandage on her left index finger. "I cut myself while shucking oysters, and believe me, the pain was all too real."

"Well, then let me put it another way," Paige replies. "Readers may experience the shattering of fictional worlds as analogous to death. Although Micaela is writing what appears to be a comic novel, it shrewdly confronts us with our own mortality. *That's* what's so damn disturbing."

There's a lull in the conversation that grows increasingly awkward, with everyone avoiding eye contact. Paula finally breaks the silence.

"Well, no offense, Paige, but I think that's a load of bull waffles. You're taking a rather silly manuscript that revels in sophomoric absurdity and endowing it with undeserved depth."

"Well, fuck you, too, Paula!" I stand up so suddenly that my wine spills and my chair crashes to the floor. "And by the way, I was lying when I said I enjoyed *The*

Heimlich Prophecies. I actually think it's banal, maudlin, mind-numbing, cliché-ridden rubbish. In the words of Dorothy Parker: 'This is not a book to be tossed aside lightly. It should be thrown with great force!'"

I grab my manuscript and storm out of the room, slamming the front door on my way out. Once outside, I pause on the front stoop, taking measured breaths while I wait for Paige to catch up so we can go home. She soon emerges, shaking her head, and opens her arms for me. I go in for the hug. Her arms are strong and comforting, and I immediately dissolve into tears.

"Don't let those boneheads get to you," Paige whispers. "They wouldn't know good writing if it bit them on the ass."

On the drive back to the bungalow, I feel increasingly angry.

"Douche bags," I say. "Whatever happened to constructive criticism?"

"Forget them. We can start our own group."

As Paige cruises down the highway, I sit in silence and stare into the headlights of the oncoming vehicles, feeling forlorn.

"I'm done writing," I say softly.

"What do you mean?"

"I've had it. I don't want to continue."

"How come?" Paige gently touches my knee. "Because those two idiots are jealous of your talent?"

"No, I'm just drained. Mentally exhausted. My imagination is tapped out, and the story is making me crazy."

"So put it away for a month or two and come back to it when you're ready."

"No, Paige, I'm done." And then an idea occurs to me. "I think you should take over."

"Huh? What do you mean?"

With every passing second my enthusiasm for this plan grows, along with my certainty that this is the right path. "You're so passionate about the story. Hell, you understand what I'm trying to do better than *I* do! So I want you to write the rest of it."

"Jesus, Micaela."

"Anyhow, you're not working on anything right now. This'll snap you out of your writer's block." It'll be good for *both* of us: I'll get the rest I need, and Paige will have a reason to write again.

"I don't know what to say." Paige pulls into her driveway and shuts off the motor.

"Then say yes."

CHAPTER TWENTY

CRYPTOPHASIA

Although I genuinely admire Micaela's manuscript, I had no intention of fulfilling her request to take over authorship of this strange tale. But Micaela was relentless in her campaign to convince me otherwise, and after three days of nonstop arguing and another three of the silent treatment, I reluctantly agreed to give it a shot, if for no other reason than to restore peace to the household.

My hesitation is multifaceted.

First, I'm uncertain whether it's feasible to take over someone else's novel and truly make it one's own. Especially a novel as idiosyncratic as this one.

Second, I am fond of Micaela, and I worry that completing her manuscript could wind up disrupting our relationship. What if Micaela isn't happy with my writing?

Third, to stay consistent, I would need to write from my subconscious, a prospect that scares the shit out of me. I tend to steer clear of introspective fiction, and always meticulously outline my plots. What sorts of inner demons might emerge if I just type whatever comes to mind?

Finally, I know damn well why my writing process has been blocked for the past six months. It started when Micaela handed out the first few chapters of her new project to the writers' group. Seeing the title of her nascent novel shook me to my core.

Incognolio! How I had fought to forget that word!

As children, Gemina—my identical twin sister—and I had made up an entire language of our own, a peculiar phenomenon that is common among twins, and technically known as cryptophasia.

In our secret language that evolved over time, when the two of us felt totally at one with each other, we called it Incognolio.

This word captured a feeling that can only be described as sheer bliss, the dissolution of all boundaries between me and Gem, the sense that we completed each other, merged into an ecstatic state of unity and fullness. Perhaps it's what we experienced when we were together in the womb.

Entering kindergarten, the two of us formed a unit that largely excluded other children. It was as if Gem and I dwelled inside a transparent cocoon, insulating us from unwanted intrusions upon our shared world, a magical place full of extraordinary imaginings and clandestine communications.

As we grew up, differences emerged in our personalities. My parents had their hearts set on raising both a boy and a girl, and although they never verbalized their disappointment in having twin girls, I somehow picked up on their disillusionment. Less secure in myself than Gem, and eager to gain my parents' approval, I became a tomboy while my sister remained very much a girly girl.

But the growing differences in our styles of dress and demeanor never disturbed the depths of our closeness. If anything, these disparities only intensified the bond. It was as if Gemina personified my feminine side while I embodied her masculinity. The resulting attraction was potent indeed, a binding force that kept us united even in the face of mounting enmity and derision from our peers as we progressed through primary and secondary schooling.

It was no surprise to anyone that we chose to attend the same college, even sharing a dorm room. Gemina majored in fine arts, focusing on painting, while I majored in philosophy. Gem wore flowing dresses and hair down to her waist, while I preferred flannel shirts, denim jeans, and closely cropped hair. Both of us considered ourselves bisexual and had various flings, but they never lasted long enough to threaten the primacy of our relationship with each other.

Gem and I had always enjoyed a relaxed physical intimacy, almost as if our bodies belonged to both of us, so it was nearly inevitable that at some point we would experiment sexually. It happened early in our sophomore year, on the night of our nineteenth birthday. Rather than spend it with friends, we decided to go out to dinner alone and splurge on an elegant French restaurant. Returning to our dorm room, tipsy from too much wine, we lay together on Gem's bed, laughing as we spoke to each other in our private language for the first time in many years.

It was Gem who recalled the term *Incognolio*, and in an attempt to recapture that glorious feeling of oneness, the two of us fell into a deep embrace. Tentatively at first, and then passionately, we kissed on the lips, nearly swooning as we each melted into the other.

Our lovemaking that night was earth-shattering, far beyond anything either of us had ever experienced before. Except for Gem's long hair, it was as if I were caressing my own mirror image, making love to myself. And yet it *wasn't* me, it was my darling sister Gemina, whom I adored more than anyone else in the world. And the awareness that this act was forbidden, that Gem and I were transgressing against the deepest of cultural taboos, only intensified our excitement and pleasure.

In the morning, hung over and sleep-deprived, the two of us barely made eye contact. We quickly parted, attending our separate classes and trying like hell to put the whole business out of mind. And yet, when we returned to our dorm room that evening, Gem and I fell upon each other like ravenous beasts, tearing off our clothes and diving back into bed, consumed with this burning need to merge, to become one.

Lovesick, drunk with ardor, reveling in the sight, the smell, the feel of our bodies, Gemina and I entered into Incognolio and neglected everything else—our friends, our studies, our ambitions—caring about nothing except our shared state of bliss. For nearly a week the two of us barely left our dorm room, except to eat. We had always loved each other, but now we were infatuated as well, unable to tolerate being apart for even a minute.

But taboos as ancient as the one prohibiting incest aren't so easily broken.

The turning point came one afternoon when Dawn, a close friend of ours, entered the dorm room without knocking, just as we were engaged in mutual cunnilingus. The look of horror and disgust on Dawn's face as she slowly backed out of the room jolted the two of us out of the stuporous spell we'd been under ever since that first kiss.

Dawn clearly couldn't keep such a juicy secret to herself, and soon our friends were avoiding us in the cafeteria. Even students whom we didn't know stared and giggled as we walked through campus.

How swiftly our shared paradise shattered, each of us blaming the other for initiating the affair. Our days of rapture morphed into a nightmare of hysterical shouting matches, petty bickering, and even a fist fight, from which we both emerged with nasty bruises and black eyes.

I finally arranged to move to another dorm across campus, and over the next several months avoided running into Gemina at all costs. So completely did I shun my sister that it was weeks after the fact that I discovered she had dropped out of school.

I was devastated. I longed for Gem unceasingly, mourning her loss like a part of me had died.

Eventually I learned to compartmentalize the pain and return to my studies. I completed my B.A. in philosophy and went on to obtain a Master's in creative writing. I married a fellow grad student who proceeded to drop out of the writing program, grow wealthy as a commodities trader, and then leave me for another woman. But the generous divorce settlement allowed me plenty of time to write. Over the next five years I managed to publish two novels—though they didn't sell particularly well, criticized by reviewers as overly tidy and intellectualized, lacking in emotional depth.

I was just starting a new novel when Micaela showed up at my writers' group with the opening pages of *Incognolio*. Upon seeing the title, I emitted an involuntary gasp. My heart fluttered and my stomach churned. A decade's worth of callousness dissolved in an instant, and longing for Gem flooded my consciousness.

I've had zero contact with my sister since she left college. Each time I come across a notice in the newspaper of a gallery showing her work, I toy with the idea of popping in, but I lack the nerve. Now, if I am to actually take over writing *Incognolio*, I have no choice. I must see Gem.

CHAPTER TWENTY-ONE

ANIMUS

I'm not ready to see my sister yet. Not by a long shot.

I have avoided psychotherapy up until now, telling myself that dwelling on the past is counterproductive. But at this point I have to admit that I need professional help.

Micaela had offered to put me in touch with her therapist, Baraka. But if I'm going to be taking over Micaela's novel, also sharing her therapist seems a bit, well…incestuous.

Lacking any other recommendations, I am hard pressed to know whom to call. So late one night, after Micaela has gone to sleep, I go through the list of psychologists in the yellow pages and listen to their phone messages, ultimately deciding to go with Dr. Heydar Ramazan, whose voice sounds compassionate and soothing, without a trace of arrogance.

I speak with him the following morning and, thanks to a cancellation, am able to see him in the afternoon.

An older man, Dr. Ramazan has a kind face and gentle manner that immediately put me at ease. Haltingly at first, but with increasing openness as the doctor lets me talk without interruption, I recount the history of my relationship with Gemina and explain why I wish to renew contact with her.

"How do you imagine Gemina might react if you were to visit her?" he asks.

"I have no idea," I reply. "That's what makes it so scary."

"What exactly do you fear?"

"That she'll refuse to talk to me, take out a restraining order, or pull out a gun."

"Holy cow. You must really be angry with her."

"*Me?* Why do you say that?"

"You have absolutely no idea what's going on in your sister's mind, Paige, and yet you imagine such extreme hostility. Could these fantasies reflect your own feelings?"

"Ah, I see. Projection." I grin. "Very astute, doctor. Well, I *am* angry. She didn't even have the decency to come to my wedding."

"Did you personally invite her?"

"No, but I mailed an invitation." I pause, looking up and to the left. "Oh, wait…um…that's right…I decided not to send it."

"Have you made *any* attempt in the last ten years to reach out to her?"

I shake my head.

"So you cut Gemina out of your life, and then blame her for not fighting her way back in?"

When I roll my eyes and slouch down in my seat, I become aware that I'm pouting.

"What if you were to visit her and find that she's glad to see you?" asks Dr. Ramazan. "Might that feel threatening as well?"

"I don't see how. I *want* us to reconcile."

"Do you, really?"

Now I'm beginning to feel irritated with this man, and wonder whether the sound of his voice might have misled me.

"I thought therapists are supposed to be supportive," I mutter. "You seem to challenge everything I say."

Dr. Ramazan laughs heartily. "Typically, I would take things at a slower pace. But I'm pushing you today, Paige, because I don't think it's likely that I'll see you again."

"Why not?"

"Because over the years you have built up such a massive wall that wards off your feelings toward Gem-

ina. I think you're terrified of exploring what lies beyond that wall."

I sit quietly for some time, looking around the office. A colorful painting catches my eye and I walk over
to it to get a better look.

It's an oil painting that suggests an interior land-
scape, a map of the psyche, reminding me of the work
of the Chilean painter, Roberto Matta. The composition
is full of mystery, conveying great beauty and immense
pain. Sure enough, Gemina's signature graces the lower
left-hand corner.

I begin weeping, overcome with the deepest grief,
and fall to my knees howling in pain, feeling like I want
to die. How I miss Gem! How I regret the lost years,
cut off from my dear sister, estranged from my very self.

Soon I feel the warmth of Dr. Ramazan's hands on
my shoulders. He gently helps me to my feet and then
holds me as I continue to cry, my entire body convuls-
ing, purging the pain I've held in so long.

When I've calmed down, we both return to our seats
and the doctor discloses that he bought the painting at
Animus, Gemina's gallery in the South End.

"I long to see her," I say softly. "I really do. But I'm
afraid...of..."

"Of what, Paige? Becoming sexually intimate again?"

I nod.

"But you were nineteen at the time. Adolescents often experiment. Don't you feel that you have greater self-control at this point?"

"I'd like to think so. But I want some assurance."

"I can't give you that, Paige. You need to trust yourself. And to do that, you must find a way to forgive yourself—and Gemina—for what happened."

With that, the session comes to a close. The doctor asks if I'd like to return next week, but I tell him that I'll call to schedule an appointment. I know he's right; I have no intention of seeing him again.

After a cup of coffee at a nearby café, I make up my mind, get back into my car, and head toward the South End, using my GPS to locate Animus.

I park and then walk around the block, stopping in at several other galleries, my heart starting to race. Perhaps I should drive home and come back another day, bringing Micaela with me to help defuse the tension.

I've already unlocked my car when I hear Gem call out my name. She's standing in front of Animus, a beseeching look on her face. After a pause, I find myself dashing across the street and into her arms.

Both of us are smiling and crying at the same time as we tightly embrace each other. Then I hold Gem at arm's length and study her face—older and sadder, yet even more beautiful than ever.

She invites me into her gallery and shows me around. Collections by several painters and sculptors are on display, each more remarkable than the next, all of them exhibiting wild flights of imagination. One corner is devoted to Gemina's work, each painting a world of its own, each one evoking the deepest mixture of feelings within me. They all seem familiar somehow, as if I had painted them in a dream.

"You're brilliant!" I tell her. "I can't even put into words how astounded I am by your talent."

Gemina smiles modestly. She compliments me on my two novels, but I can tell that she was disappointed by them.

Gem brews chai tea and the two of us sit and talk, occasionally interrupted by customers who have questions about some of the artworks, a couple of them making purchases.

At closing time, I invite Gem to dinner at my house, and Micaela joins the two of us out on the deck for cocktails.

"I can't get over how alike the two of you look," Micaela says. "And yet your personalities are so different." Then Micaela asks Gemina whether she has a partner, and I can't help noticing a trace of flirtatiousness in her voice.

"I've had various boyfriends and girlfriends, but no one at present." Gem smiles. "I tend to get bored too easily."

After dinner, Gem and I go for a walk along the beach. I pour my heart out to her—expressing how confused I was by our sexual affair, how much I've missed her, how lonely I've been these past years—while she listens with compassionate interest.

It's fantastic to get all this off my chest, and I feel wonderfully close to Gem, walking along the sea hand in hand. Only one thing dampens my high spirits: Gem repeatedly asks me to tell her more about Micaela.

CHAPTER TWENTY-TWO

FLIP, SIP, OR STRIP

For the next couple of weeks, Gemina, Micaela, and I are inseparable. Gem arranges to have her assistant take over at Animus, and I put Gem up in my second guest room.

The three of us spend our days at the beach, sunbathing, swimming, kayaking, and sailing. In the evenings, we have cocktails on the deck, go out for dinner, hang out at a local jazz club, then head home to drink some more, smoke weed, and talk and laugh into the wee hours.

With each passing day I grow more jealous of the intimacy that has developed between my sister and Micaela, but I'm so thrilled to have Gem back in my life that I do what I can to suppress the disagreeable feelings.

One night, unable to get to sleep, I tiptoe into Gemina's room and slip into bed beside her. For a while I just lie there watching her sleep, her breathing so gentle and childlike, her face angelic in the moonlight. Absentmindedly, I begin to stroke her long blond hair, sleek and silken to my touch.

"Who's that?" Gem mutters, stirring.

"It's me," I whisper. "I can't get to sleep."

"What's wrong?"

"I dunno," I say. Then, without thinking, I blurt out, "Are you falling in love with Micaela?"

"What?"

"I see the way you look at her, Gem. I know something's going on."

Gemina, now fully awake, searches my eyes.

"I don't know, Paige. I suppose I've got a bit of a crush. She's an intriguing woman."

I sigh and turn away, shifting to my back. Gemina reaches out and caresses my cheek.

"It doesn't change anything between us," she says. "I'll always love you best."

I remain silent and sullen, thinking dark thoughts.

Gemina softly kisses me on the forehead.

I begin to cry, blubbering, "It's just that I've missed you so much. I want you all to myself."

She smiles sadly, and her tears fall onto my face.

Impulsively, I raise my head and kiss her full on the lips, breathing in her familiar scent.

Gemina pulls back. "Careful, Paige. This is dangerous territory."

"I don't care. I don't want to lose you." I draw Gem to me and kiss her hard, running my hand down the curves of her body.

Gemina breaks away from my embrace. "So control yourself. If you don't want to lose me, then we can't risk getting sexually involved. It's that simple."

I want to argue back, but I know that she's right. Instead, I sulk, and eventually return to my own bed.

I sleep badly and wake up with a sore neck. Thinking back on what happened in Gem's bed, I realize that I acted foolishly, but still resent my sister for pushing me away.

Breakfast is awkward. I feel like the proverbial third wheel, silently sipping coffee as Micaela and Gem flirt and laugh, having a grand old time.

I decide not to go to the beach with them, and they don't put up much of a fight. Instead, I try to work on *Incognolio*, but I'm too pissed off to concentrate. Now I wonder why the hell I thought reconciling with Gemina would make it easier to write.

Instead, I go for a long walk to clear my head. I tell myself that I've sexualized my wish to be close to my sister. Being intimate doesn't mean having to fuck her.

And it doesn't necessarily mean merging with her. In-cognolio was fine when we were young kids with flu-id boundaries and magical thinking. Now, we're adult women, and adults don't merge.

By cocktail time, I've managed to straighten myself out and no longer feel so angry. The three of us drink piña coladas as we listen to reggae and tell funny stories.

At dinner in town the wine flows freely, and by the time we get back home everyone's stewed. Gem and Micaela are hanging all over each other and even ex-changing little pecks on the cheek. I egg them on to prove I've transcended my petty jealousy, but in the back of my mind, I'm wondering whether Gem might agree to a threesome.

Sitting on pillows on the living room floor, I say, "I know. Let's play Flip, Sip, or Strip!"

"What's that?" asks Micaela.

"Okay, so we each take turns calling a coin flip." I take a quarter out of my pocket. "If you guess right, pass the coin to your right. If you guess wrong, pass the coin to your left and either remove something you're wearing or take a shot."

Gem and Micaela both giggle.

"There's one catch," I add. "You can't do the same thing—sip or strip—more than twice in a row."

They excitedly agree to the game, so I fetch three shot glasses and a bottle of Cuervo Gold from the liquor cabinet and get started, flipping the quarter, guessing wrong, and taking off my shoes.

"Anything that's a pair counts as one item," I point out.

Before long, shoes, earrings, necklaces, pants, blouses, and dresses are all in a pile, and the three of us are sitting in our underwear, getting increasingly drunk.

Micaela is the first to remove her bra, which she does tantalizingly, like a professional stripper, accompanied by oohs and ahs. Several shots later, Gem and I are also topless.

By the time all three of us are bare assed, I'm flying high, and feeling optimistic about my chances of initiating a ménage à trois. When Micaela excuses herself to go to the bathroom, I sidle over to Gem, whom I haven't seen naked since our college days, and kiss her lovely neck.

If I weren't so smashed I'd feel Gem tense up, but oblivious to her feelings and intoxicated by the scent of her sweet flesh, I run my hands over my sister's body and take her left nipple into my mouth.

"Cut it out!" Gem shoves me away and scowls. "I *told* you I don't want to get into that."

Anguished and humiliated, I stand up and stumble out of the living room and out onto the deck without stopping to put my clothes back on. I stare up at the sky, the mad swarm of stars making me dizzy and nauseous.

Impulsively I stagger down the stairs and across the beach to throw myself into the sea. Over and over I plunge my head underwater, determined to drown myself, to end the misery for once and for all.

But I can't do it. Coughing and sputtering, I finally crawl back and collapse on the sand, disgusted with my inability to even kill myself. I cry like a baby as I drift into unconsciousness.

A short time later, awakened by the rising tide, I manage to get to my feet and stumble back into the bungalow. I find the living room empty and wonder where Gem and Micaela have gone. Muffled noises coming from down the hall prompt me to open the door to Micaela's room, where I discover the two of them making love.

Gripped by a wild fury, I grab a carving knife from the kitchen and stagger back to the guest room, an animal-like growl escaping from the depths of my gut.

"I'll kill you!" I shout, seizing Gem by the hair and holding the knife to her throat. "You traitor! You cunt!"

Gem is frozen in terror. Micaela pleads with me to put the knife down.

I'm on the verge of slicing Gem open when her eyes meet mine and my heart breaks. Sobbing, I lower the knife and let go of Gem's hair.

Still clutching the carving knife, buzzing on adrenaline and crazed with emotion, I order the two of them out of bed and into the living room. Gem makes as if to put on her clothes, but I stop her, saying, "No. Nobody gets dressed." I have Micaela sit on the sofa while Gemina and I sit facing each other on the floor, chest to chest, hugging each other tightly.

"The time has arrived for the two to become one," I announce, my voice sounding drugged and hypnotic. "Join me in chanting the sacred word, so that Gem and Paige may merge and remain together from this night on."

I begin chanting, "Incognolio...incognolio...incognolio..."

"Cut it out," says Micaela. "You're scaring us."

Without releasing Gem, I retrieve the knife from the floor and jab the point lightly into my sister's side. "Chant with me, Micaela! You too, Gem, or I swear to God I'll kill you."

Both now join me, their voices shaky, all three of us intoning, "Incognolio...incognolio...incognolio...incognolio."

After several minutes, the lights in the room begin to flicker, a low rumbling grows louder, and the stench of burning rubber fills the air. A strange tingling sensation courses through my body, and I'm convinced that the miracle has occurred.

When I open my eyes, the first thing I see is Micaela perched on the sofa, a look of sheer horror on her face. Gem shrieks and tries to pull away from me but can't. I turn my head and find that my cheek is somehow stuck to hers. Starting to panic, I ask Gem to stand, and the two of us struggle to our feet.

And now it's all too clear what's happened. Our torsos are fused. We are conjoined.

CHAPTER TWENTY-THREE

MAZAZEL

The next morning, I'm having breakfast out on the deck with Paige. The sunshine is glorious, and cumulous clouds drift majestically across an azure sky, like swans across a lake.

"I'm sorry, Micaela, but I can't take over your novel," Paige says. "I tried my damnedest, but I just can't seem to write."

"That's cool," I say. "I had a breakthrough last night. Words came pouring out nonstop."

"Excellent. Glad to hear it."

"Yeah, except some scary shit surfaced. You had this identical twin sister you loved so much that you wanted to merge with her, and the two of you ended up conjoined."

"Holy crap." Paige shakes her head. "How do you come up with this stuff?"

I shrug my shoulders.

"Speaking of which, I've been meaning to ask how you came up with the title for your novel."

"Oh, that." I choke on a bite of toast and Paige pats me on the back until I stop coughing. "It's…really not that interesting."

Paige cocks her head, clearly wondering why I don't seem to want to talk about it. I am indeed reticent, but after some thought, figure maybe it would be good to talk it over with someone.

"It's actually pretty freaky," I say. "See, I was taking this novel-writing workshop at the adult education center. There were eight of us in the class, all trying to get going on a novel. Phil, the instructor, told us that if we don't know where to begin, we can start by developing a specific character, a setting, a theme, a dialogue, a first line, or even a title.

"I thought it might be fun to start with just a title. So the following afternoon, sipping a cappuccino at Brew Ha Ha, I jotted down a bunch of possible titles, none of which I liked. Then it occurred to me to try using a nonsense word, so I generated a list of about twenty of them, off the top of my head.

"Looking back over the list, two of the words stood out: Incognolio and Mazazel. I was trying to decide which one I liked best when a middle-aged man appeared and asked if he might sit down across from me. I said sure, even though there were several empty tables in the café."

"None of this sounds freaky to me," Paige interrupts.

"Just wait 'til you hear what happened next," I say. "So this guy introduced himself as Misha Slodkin, and said that he needed to speak to me about something of tremendous importance. 'I know you are writing a novel,' he said. 'I'm here to tell you that this novel will dramatically change the world.'"

"Jesus," says Paige.

"I know," I reply. "I laughed out loud and asked him whether my friend, Dean, had put him up to it, but he said he was deadly serious. He told me that my novel would become wildly popular, outselling even the Bible."

"I like the sound of that," says Paige.

"That's what *I* said. But Slodkin didn't see the humor. He said that the impact of my novel on the direction of humankind would be unprecedented, but whether it was for good or for ill all depended on my choice of a title.

"When I asked him why so much hinged on the title, he said that depending upon the title I chose, a completely different novel would emerge from my unconscious. Then he reached for the list of nonsense words I'd composed, with Incognolio and Mazazel underlined. At this point, Slodkin became agitated."

Paige leans forward, her eyes alight.

"He said, 'If you choose *Incognolio* as your title, the future of humanity is bright. There will be peace and prosperity among all nations, people will learn to accept and celebrate their differences, the culture of corporate greed will be replaced by a culture that values individual freedom and opportunity, civil rights for everyone, and responsible stewardship of the environment.'

"Then Slodkin's face turned pale. He said, 'But if you choose *Mazazel* as the title of your novel, dark days are in store for our planet. Selfishness, hostility, and greed shall flourish—man against man, and nation against nation. A Third World War will wipe out the vast majority of humans, decimate the cities and countryside, and contaminate the entire globe with nuclear radiation, setting off mass extinctions of plant and animal species.'"

"All because of the title of your novel?" asks Paige. She leans back in her chair and crosses her arms. "That's absurd."

"That's exactly what I told him, Paige. Then I said, 'Even if it's true, how could you possibly know all of this?' and he said: 'Because I'm from the future.' Well, I had a good chuckle over that, and was now nearly certain this was one of Dean's practical jokes.

"To make a long story a bit shorter, I played along with Slodkin, and assured him that I'd title the novel

Incognolio. But when I ran into Dean a couple of days later, he swore up and down that he had nothing to do with the incident at Brew Ha Ha. Which left me wondering, as ridiculous as it sounded, what if Misha Slodkin was really from the future?"

Paige raises an eyebrow at this.

"So, just in case, I went with *Incognolio*. But as I proceeded with the manuscript, something started bugging me. I kept thinking back on the appearance of Slodkin's face. There was a look in his eyes, a subtle hint of duplicity that left me feeling suspicious of his true intentions.

"I began to wonder: what if he misled me? What if naming the novel *Mazazel* would lead to the idyllic scenario, and by going with *Incognolio* I was dooming humanity to a hellish future?

"And in fact, although I set out to write a comic novel, the manuscript has grown increasingly dark and morbid. So, lately, I've been thinking of starting over from scratch, and calling it *Mazazel*."

"Really, Micaela?" Paige gives me the stink eye. "A man from the future? And don't you think it's just a little grandiose of you to believe that your novel could have such an extraordinary impact on history?"

I break out laughing and admit that I made the whole thing up.

"Why?" asks Paige, looking hurt.

"I'm sorry," I say. "But the real story is...sort of embarrassing."

With a hint of wariness, Paige gestures for me to continue.

"Well, I'd become so miserable being married to Jack that I got back into heavy drug use. I progressed from pain killers to cocaine to crystal meth, and eventually was mainlining heroin. I felt disgusted with myself, and when a friend mentioned that hypnosis can help with addiction, I decided to give it a shot.

"I started seeing a psychologist who was trained in hypnosis, and she was focusing on relaxation training, emotional clearing, and post-hypnotic suggestion. But when I didn't make much progress, she said we needed to do some exploratory work, involving a deeper level of trance.

"One afternoon in her office, while I was so far under that I was barely conscious, I started speaking in a strange, foreign-sounding accent. I was apparently channeling a disembodied entity who called itself Quodon. This entity claimed to be one of my spirit guides, and it declared that I was in imminent danger of what it called *soul death*. I lost all awareness at that point, but my hypnotherapist later told me that Quodon announced that the only thing that could save me from oblivion was to write a novel in which I gave my subconscious mind free rein. Quodon also insisted that I must call the novel—"

"Micaela," Paige interrupts, looking at me with disappointment in her eyes. "You're making up this story, too, aren't you?"

I sigh heavily and then nod.

"Why are you doing this, Micaela?" asks Paige. "I feel like you don't trust me."

"It's not that. Not at all. I swear, Paige! It's just that…I can't remember where the title came from."

"Can't remember?"

"Not a clue. In fact, when you get right down to it, I can't really remember *anything* that happened to me prior to starting the novel."

Paige has a curious look on her face.

"What are you thinking?" I ask.

"Well, now that you mention it, I have no memory of *my* life prior to joining the writers' group."

The two of us sit in silence, staring at each other.

"So what does it all mean?" I ask.

"Don't you see?" Paige replies in a hushed tone somewhere between reverence and horror. "We're not real. We're characters in a novel."

CHAPTER TWENTY-FOUR

ANGELICA

Even while submerged in the depths of depression, I couldn't resist the joke of writing myself into the previous chapter, appearing in Micaela's fabricated story as the Man from the Future.

If only, I think to myself, I could actually *live* in the future—or the past, for that matter—anywhere but the wretched present.

The present, in which I live alone in a decrepit studio apartment, barely getting by on the meager Social Security disability payments I receive due to my intractable depression. The present, in which I continue to grieve the loss of my wife, Angelica, who died in childbirth last year. Yes, the present, in which I try to keep myself from going crazy by working on a book titled *Incognolio*, a story that started out as a comic novel, but with every page seems to grow increasingly dark and disturbing. In retrospect, I suppose this should not be surprising, given the circumstances that inspired the novel.

After suffering through three miscarriages in as many years, Angelica became pregnant once again. This time she turned to an acupuncturist who specialized in treating infertile and pregnant women, from whom she also purchased a Chinese fertility charm in the shape of a fish, which she placed on the mantle in our living room.

Since the three miscarriages had all occurred relatively early in pregnancy, by the time Angelica was six months along, the two of us began to feel more confident that this time she would carry to term. An ultrasound had revealed that she was carrying twins, a boy and a girl. Angelica chose the name Micaela for the girl, and I settled on Muldoon for the boy.

The pregnancy progressed without a hitch, except that Angelica's due date came and went. After several days passed, Dr. Menos booked her a room in the hospital, and the next morning she induced delivery. After a long day of labor on a busy ward, Angelica developed a strep infection. Dr. Menos reassured the two of us that this was a common complication, and prescribed ampicillin.

Although my wife had no history of allergies, she immediately suffered a massive anaphylactic reaction, her blood pressure dropping precipitously, her lips swelling up and turning blue. But despite all their efforts at resuscitation, her condition deteriorated. An emergency C-section was performed. Both twins were stillborn. Angelica died shortly thereafter.

As the doctor delivered her heartfelt condolences, I remained in a state of shock and barely said a word to the social worker who met with me. Afterward, I stopped in at a tavern and sat at the bar, drinking shot after shot of whiskey until the bartender cut me off.

Unsteady on my feet, I left and wandered through the city streets until I came to the harbor. I walked along a beach and then stood facing the ocean, watching the waves come in. There was a black hole where my heart used to be. I was furious at God and began cursing him, shouting like a madman. Then I fell down and cried, weeping and wailing as I clawed at the sand.

But the pain was too much, too overwhelming, and suddenly I knew what I had to do. I stood up and stumbled into the water, still bawling like a baby. When I was neck-deep, I shrieked a final *fuck you* at God and plunged my head underwater. My chest heaved as I continued to cry, and I swallowed mouthful after mouthful of the sea. I surfaced briefly, coughing and spluttering, and then thrust my head underwater once more, this time determined to finish the job. The dead silence underwater was eerie, but just before I blacked out I distinctly heard a single word spoken.

A man who was taking a late-night stroll on the boardwalk had heard me cursing at God. He managed to pull me out of the water and successfully administer mouth-to-mouth resuscitation.

After three weeks on a psychiatric ward and a course of twelve electroconvulsive treatments, I was deemed well enough to return home. But I still felt too depressed and dejected to continue working as a clinical psychologist. I decided to go on leave, and despite the earnest pleadings of my patients, bid farewell and transferred them to other therapists working at my clinic.

Without a salary, living only on disability payments and what remained of a small savings account, I could no longer afford the spacious two-bedroom condo I'd shared with Angelica and moved to a tiny studio apartment in the poorest neighborhood of the city.

My grief for Angelica and the dead twins was unbearable, and the only thing that pulled me out of my despair was the memory of the word I heard before I nearly drowned, spoken in a voice that was transcendently beautiful. I was convinced that the word held some profound meaning, a meaning that I had to discover within myself. Although I'd never written fiction before, I decided to try my hand at a novel, starting only with the title, *Incognolio*.

CHAPTER TWENTY-FIVE

LASZLO SKUNTCH

Figuring that Incognolio emerged from the depths of my unconscious, I've written whatever has come to mind, censoring nothing. But now, after writing every day for several months, I feel no closer to comprehending the enigmatic word. Clearly, it's time to attempt a different approach.

What if, I wonder, I'm not the only person who has been visited by Incognolio? Could it be that I am meant to get in touch with this other person or persons? It seems worth a try. So I place a notice in the personals section of Craigslist and the local newspaper, asking anyone who has heard of Incognolio to contact me.

In the first few days, all I get are a couple of crank calls from morons who saw my phone number in the paper. Undeterred, I post the notice every day for an entire month. Still no luck.

I'm ready to give up when, on a hunch, I decide to keep running the ad with the word *Mazazel* substituted for *Incognolio*. And on the seventeenth day, I receive an email that reads:

Dear Dr. Slodkin,

I am responding to your post, and am intrigued to hear from someone who has knowledge of Mazazel. If you are serious about this inquiry, please meet me tonight at The Drunken Duck, at ten o'clock sharp. I shall be wearing a black beret.

Sincerely,
Laszlo Skuntch

I am elated, certain that I'm now on the right track. I reply to the email, confirming our meeting, and head out that evening feeling hopeful, eager to meet the man in the black beret. At precisely 10:00 PM I arrive at The Drunken Duck, just a short walk from my apartment. When I enter, I spot Laszlo Skuntch almost immediately, sitting at a booth with his back toward me.

I walk over and sit down across from him and am about to introduce myself when my jaw drops open.

Laszlo appears equally bewildered. Once he recovers himself, he says, "Misha Slodkin, I presume?"

"Yes!" I say. "*B-B-Brother?*"

"It would appear that way."

Except for the beret, a pencil-line mustache, and a malevolent gleam in his eyes, it's as if I'm looking in the mirror.

It turns out that both of us knew that we'd been adopted at birth, but neither had ever been told about having a biological sibling, let alone an identical twin.

"I'm stunned," I say. "But perhaps on some level I knew all along. That would help explain why the novel I'm writing is crawling with twins."

"I'm working on a novel as well," Laszlo replies. "That's why I responded to your notice. You see, my novel is titled *Mazazel*."

"No kidding! Mine is titled *Incognolio*, but one of my characters almost titles *her* novel *Mazazel*."

"Astonishing."

A waitress stops by and we both order Jack Daniels on the rocks, which she swiftly delivers. I tell Laszlo about how I lost Angelica and the twins, and then heard the word *Incognolio* when I was on the verge of drowning.

Laszlo conveys his condolences. But when I ask him how he came up with the title of his novel, he abruptly changes the subject. This only whets my curiosity, however, and I repeatedly press him until he relents.

"Fine." His voice is now hushed. "But you must promise *never* to repeat this story to anyone. Is that clear?"

"I promise, I promise. Word of honor."

Laszlo scrutinizes me and then says, "Very well." He tosses off his whiskey and signals the waitress for another round.

"Like many couples who adopt their first child, my parents—who had given up all hope of having a child of their own—conceived my brother within months of my arrival. Kurt was just a year younger than me, and I despised the little prick from the moment I laid eyes on him.

"My parents did nothing to hide the fact that they loved Kurt more than me, that they regarded him as their true son, whereas I was simply an intruder. Kurt's birthdays were grand celebrations, while mine were barely acknowledged. Kurt's Christmas presents were extravagant, while mine were chintzy at best. Kurt was enrolled at the finest private academies, while I languished in our town's woefully underfunded public school system."

The waitress brings our drinks, and Laszlo tells her to keep them coming.

"Do you know what it's like to be treated as a second-class citizen? As an interloper?" he asks me.

"No," I reply. "I grew up without siblings."

"Well, it was hell, let me tell you. I repeatedly ran away but was always dragged back home, where my father, who never missed an opportunity to beat the stuffing out of me, welcomed me with a thorough thrashing.

"Anyhow, Kurt—the golden child—went on to graduate from Princeton and Harvard Medical School, tuition paid in full by my parents, who gave not one penny toward my college degree. Kurt became a pediatric surgeon, the best in his field, whereas I became an entrepreneur, starting up a series of businesses that unfailingly failed, leaving me nearly penniless. Kurt married his childhood sweetheart and had three adorable children and a golden retriever, while I lived friendless and alone.

"Last year I received an invitation from Kurt to join him and his family on Christmas day. This came as somewhat of a surprise, given that we had been largely out of touch since the demise of our parents. Nevertheless, I accepted the invitation.

"From the moment I arrived, I was suffused with envy. In stark contrast to my hovel in town, Kurt's suburban mansion was opulent. Kurt's wife was gracious and gorgeous, and his children were charming and full of life, laughing and joking as they opened their presents. Always thoughtful and considerate to a fault, Kurt had left an expensive gift for me under the tree. But that only fueled my resentment, reminding me of the gross disparity in the Christmas presents we'd received as kids.

"By the time we finished supper, I was seething with anger and bitterness. Kurt had all the advantages growing up, and now he possessed everything I longed for, while I had nothing.

"While my sister-in-law cleaned up and the kids played with their new toys, Kurt invited me to share some fine Cognac out on the back porch. We stood at the railing, looking out on his enormous wooded yard, which was covered with more than a foot of glistening snow. Huge icicles hung from the eaves, slowly melting in the bright December sun.

"Sipping his Courvoisier, Kurt waxed poetic about the beauty and wonder of life. He rhapsodized about how fulfilling his work was, describing his recent trip to Zimbabwe, where he helped set up medical clinics in some of the most destitute regions of that impoverished nation. When he returned home he realized more than ever how fortunate he was to have such a rewarding life, and such a loving wife and family.

"As my brother droned on, I gulped down the Cognac and worked myself into a frenzy of mounting fury. Each and every day he saved the lives of *children*, for Christ's sake, whereas I offered nothing to society, caring only for myself. Had he no idea how smug and superior he sounded? Had he no inkling of how agonizingly envious and resentful I felt?

"I wanted to scream at Kurt, to strangle him. A dark force welled up within me that I could no longer contain. Placing my empty snifter upon the railing, I was on the verge of attacking my brother when my eye caught the sparkle of the largest of the icicles looming above us. In a flash, I jumped up and snapped it off. Cupping the back of Kurt's head with one hand, I used the other to jam the pointed end of my weapon into his eye and deep into his brain, just as I heard a voice within me—sinister and vicious—shout out: *Mazazel!*"

Laszlo sees the horror in my eyes and can't quite manage to keep his lips from curling into a grin.

"Did Kurt die?" I ask.

"Instantly. I told his wife that we'd been looking up and admiring the icicles when one of them broke loose and pierced his eye. Of course, there were no fingerprints, and by the time the police arrived the murder weapon was nothing but a pool of water. Why, I couldn't have devised a more devious means of killing him if I'd planned it for months in advance!"

CHAPTER TWENTY-SIX

PRESIDENT DORK

"I can see that my story has made quite an impression on you," says Laszlo, who now smiles broadly. "Well, before you get up and run out of here, I suppose I should inform you that none of it is true."

"What do you mean?" I ask.

"I made the whole thing up just now! That's what I do, Misha. I'm a crime novelist."

"So you didn't kill Kurt?"

"Kurt doesn't exist. Like you, I grew up as an only child."

Feeling rattled, I take a drink of whiskey. On the one hand, I'm relieved that my twin brother isn't a maniacal murderer. On the other, I now mistrust him and wonder why he would play such morbid mind games.

"You're a strange man, Laszlo," I say. "And you still haven't told me how you came up with the title of your novel."

"The truth of the matter is that the real story is so bizarre that you'll never believe it."

"Try me," I say.

"I was scheduled to have a cavity filled this morning, so I went to Dr. Horniak's office in the Medical Arts building. I entered the elevator and pressed the button for the sixth floor. When the doors opened, I thought I was on the wrong floor, since the carpet in the hallway was blue instead of beige. So I pressed the button for six again, but the elevator didn't budge. Figuring they had replaced the carpet, I walked down the hallway, but I couldn't shake the feeling that something was wrong. Upon entering suite 639, there was a secretary at the desk whom I didn't recognize. When I told her that I had a two-thirty appointment, she burst out laughing."

"How come?" I ask Laszlo.

"She said it was a gynecology practice! Scratching my head, I pointed out that Grunyon Horniak's name was still on the office door, and she replied that Dr. Horniak was the gynecologist. I said I was certain that he was a dentist, but the secretary insisted that she had been working in that same office for several years.

"I took the elevator back to the lobby and left the building. Feeling distraught, I went around the corner to get a whiskey at Dirty Nelly's, but the pub was gone and there was a post office in its place!"

As he traced one side of his mustache with the tip of a finger, Laszlo searched my eyes, probably wondering whether I'd guessed where this was headed.

"Well, I needed stamps to pay my bills, so I went in to buy some. While I was paying for the stamps, I noticed a framed photo of the host of *You're Fired!* on the wall. I asked the woman who was assisting me why there was a picture of that asswipe—Donald J. Dork—in a U.S. post office, and when she said he was the president, it finally dawned on me that I'd entered an alternate universe."

"Okay, Laszlo," I say. "I've had enough of this. If you don't want to tell me how you came up with your title that's fine, but spare me your idiot tales."

"See, I told you you'd never believe me. But I swear to God it's the truth!"

"Right." I study him for tells and find none, which convinces me that, at the very least, *he* believes what he's saying. I heave a sigh and settle back into my chair. "So finish the damn story."

"I like to think I'm the adventurous type, Misha. But I really couldn't stomach a reality in which Dork was the leader of the free world. So I headed back to what was now labeled the Medical Arts & Crafts building, figuring that the elevator had to be the portal between universes. I took the elevator up to the sixth floor, hoping to get back home, but the carpet was still blue. I rode up and down repeatedly, but no luck.

"I walked down the street and bought a paper at a newsstand to at least see what was going on in this world, and then hailed a cab, directing the cabby to what I hoped was still my apartment. En route, I came across a photo of myself in the newspaper. The accompanying article said that there was a rumor circulating the Internet that the famous crime novelist, Laszlo Skuntch, was a serial killer. Someone had apparently gone through a list of the unsolved murder cases in the city over the past fifteen years, and discovered a pattern. According to the rumor, for each novel I published, I conducted 'research' by murdering someone in the exact same way that the killer knocks off his victim in my book!

"Needless to say, I found this disturbing, although not altogether surprising, given that in my home universe I'm a professional hit man."

"Say what?" I say.

"I'm a freelance hit man, Misha. Folks pay me to terminate someone they want dead. Anyhow, I got home and everything seemed to be the same as usual, except that my pit bull, Boudreaux, was missing and for some reason I owned an African Grey parrot who kept calling me *fuckface*.

"I immediately went to my computer to check my email and get oriented. There I discovered a message from someone named Floreska, who is apparently my literary agent. She indicated that she didn't believe the allegations that I was the Mystery Murderer, but that even if they were true, the publicity would be a boon for book sales. Floreska also asked whether I'd finished *Mazazel*, the novel I'd just started writing in my home universe.

"I accessed my files, opened one called *Mazazel*, and skimmed the manuscript, which in fact is not finished. Then I returned to my emails and discovered one from you, confirming our ten o'clock meeting at the Drunken Duck. Well, as the protagonist in *Mazazel*, *I* have an important meeting at the Drunken Duck, so I figured that I'd better go. I had dinner, fed the goddamn parrot, threw on a black beret, and here I am."

I am silent for some time, wondering what to make of this outlandish account.

Finally, I say, "So you're suggesting that I exist in the alternate universe you've stumbled into?"

"Precisely," Laszlo replies. "And you're also a character in the book I'm writing. As soon as I saw your face it all made sense."

"How do you mean?"

"You see, *Mazazel* is another crime novel." Laszlo smiles, his eyes radiating pure evil. "The story is about a man who murders his long-lost twin brother."

CHAPTER TWENTY-SEVEN

LUNARIA

"You're not seriously planning to kill me, are you?" I ask Laszlo, not knowing what to believe at this point.

"It all depends on how I decide to murder you in my novel," he replies. "As a hit man, I've used just about every lethal method that's been devised. But if I happen to come up with something new...well, let's just say you'd better watch your back."

"But why is it necessary to try out a method before you write about it? It's just a book, for Christ's sake."

"Authenticity, my dear brother." Laszlo grins. "Since I appear to be trapped in this universe, I've decided to pick up where the other Laszlo left off, and my readers demand no less than complete believability."

I roll my eyes and then get up to leave. Laszlo tosses some bills on the table to cover the drinks and accompanies me to the door.

"By the way," he says, "how the hell did Dork manage to make it to the White House?"

"Motherfucker assembled a massively-armed Tea-Party militia," I reply. "Staged a military coup."

"Jesus," says Laszlo. He bids me farewell and I start walking back to my apartment, vowing never to place another damn ad in Craigslist.

The more I think about him, the more I despise Laszlo. In general, I'm an amicable fellow who hardly ever feels ill will toward anyone. As a psychotherapist, I treated some mighty disturbed folks, but always managed to find something to like about them. With Laszlo, though, I am filled with unadulterated loathing and revulsion, and can find no redeeming trait whatsoever.

As I walk, I'm aware of how disorienting it feels to regard myself as dwelling in someone else's alternate universe. I like to think that *my* universe is the real universe, and any others that might be out there exist as alternates, and are thus subordinate in status. But now I see that this view is irrational, a symptom of universe-centric thinking, and that my home universe is no better or more central than any other.

As I ponder how many alternate universes may contain some version of me, a familiar voice calls out, "Dr. Slodkin!"

"Lunaria!" I reply, feeling both excitement and trepidation.

Lunaria, an exceedingly beautiful and neurotic woman in her thirties, is one of my former patients. I know it would be best to just greet her and continue on my way, but she stands directly in my path, arms crossed, defying me to avoid a conversation with her.

"What are you doing out so late?" she asks.

"Had a drink with someone," I respond. "And yourself?"

"I'm attending a Wakan at a nearby loft. You should come along."

Wakans, spiritual gatherings that begin at midnight and last until dawn, have recently become all the rage. Akin to the Native American peyote ceremony, the Wakan was designed to allow participants to commune with the spirit world.

"Are you sure that would be good for you?"

"Are you whacked?" Lunaria replies. "Attending Wakans has been a life saver for me! Especially since *you* fucking dumped me."

Four years ago, when she first entered treatment, I knew Lunaria was going to be a handful. She was flirtatious, demanding, and manipulative, and she rapidly developed a powerful transference that alternated between adoring me and treating me like shit.

I had dealt with similar patient-therapist dynamics in the past and managed to use them to promote the therapeutic process, but this time it was different. I first noticed it in small things, like my paying more attention to how I dressed on the days that I was scheduled to see Lunaria. I bent the rules, allowing her to continue talking for several minutes after sessions had ended, and letting her owe her co-payments month after month without addressing the issue.

Soon I became aware that I was thinking about Lunaria between sessions to an inordinate degree. I had become infatuated with her. Normally I refrained from discussing my work with Angelica, to whom I was engaged at the time, but in this instance, I felt compelled to reveal what was going on, almost as if I felt guilty of infidelity. This only made matters worse, since Angelica became jealous of my feelings toward Lunaria. She asked me to transfer her to another therapist, which I refused to do, insisting that it would be too traumatic for my patient. Instead, partly in an effort to assuage Angelica's jealousy, I set a date for our wedding.

Once we were married, I would slip off my wedding band before Lunaria's sessions, afraid of how she might react to seeing it. This went on for well over a year until, one day, I forgot to replace the ring afterwards. When I showed up at home with my finger bare, Angelica guessed what was going on. Furious, she made me promise to end the deception.

The next session, as soon as Lunaria spotted the ring, she became enraged. She cursed me up and down, screaming at me one moment and sobbing the next. Lunaria accused me of humiliating and betraying her, of leading her on just so I could inflict the deepest pain.

That evening she tried to kill herself by washing down an entire month's worth of Lucidazole with a bottle of Southern Comfort. I was interrupted by a call during a night out with Angelica, and I left her sitting alone at Fleur de Lis while I rushed to the hospital where Lunaria was having her stomach pumped.

After that episode, I could no longer kid myself that continuing to treat Lunaria was in her best interest. Instead, I began talking to her about ending the treatment and referring her to another therapist. Lunaria would have none of it. She pleaded and cajoled, insisting that the therapy was helping her. She threatened to make another suicide attempt. She even attended one session wearing a short skirt and no panties, slouching down in her seat so as to give me a clear view of her snatch.

Finally, I realized that I couldn't justify the termination purely in terms of what was best for Lunaria, a proposition that she would never accept. In our final session, I told Lunaria that for personal reasons I could no longer continue being her therapist, and referred her to Dr. Freeman. When Lunaria asked me to elaborate, I began to cry. Unable to contain my emotions, I wept as I admitted that I had fallen in love with her. Lunaria stared at me, tears running down her face, and then ran out of my office, never to return.

"Don't you like Dr. Freeman?" I ask her now.

"Only saw him once. When you've had the best, Misha, there's no going back."

"That's ridiculous," I say, feeling both flattered and irritated. "Anyhow, with your history of drug addiction, don't you think it's risky to be fooling around with Anosh?"

Anosh, a psychedelic agent extracted from the adrenal glands of the Bolivian marmoset, was ingested during the Wakan.

"It's totally safe," Lunaria insists. "It's nothing like heroin or meth. It puts you in touch with ultimate reality."

I am unsuccessful in my attempts to change Lunaria's mind, and finally decide to accompany her to the ceremony in order to provide assistance should she happen to unravel psychologically.

At least that's how I rationalize this decision to myself.

CHAPTER TWENTY-EIGHT

WAKAN

As we enter the loft apartment where the Wakan is to take place, we find the air laden with incense—a heady mixture of sandalwood, sage, and myrrh. The light in the expansive room is soft and dim, produced by dozens of candles of every size, shape, and color. In the background, I can hear the low drone of an Indian tambura.

Lunaria and I are greeted by the Shazan—the ceremonial leader—a wizened woman who somehow appears ageless, with smiling eyes and a profoundly peaceful aura.

There are about twenty participants sitting cross-legged on pillows in a large circle, most of them in their late teens and twenties. An air of breathless anticipation fills the room, as if something miraculous is about to occur.

When everyone is settled, the Shazan indicates that anyone who is having second thoughts about taking part in the Wakan should leave immediately, since once the ceremony begins we will be required to remain there until sunrise.

People glance around at one another, but no one gets up to leave. Although I don't intend to ingest the Anosh, I feel committed to looking after Lunaria and making sure that no harm comes to her.

"Good," says the Shazan. "Then we shall begin."

She strikes the small gong sitting in front of her with a wooden mallet, and everyone sits rapt as the mellow tone rings out, gradually fades, and finally disappears.

"Oh, Great Spirit, whose breath gives life to the universe, may you bless this Wakan," says the old woman. "Creator of All, we welcome you into our hearts, minds, bodies, and souls. We humbly ask you to guide our journey into the spirit world. Let the illusory world fall away, allowing us to perceive the timeless reality of the Nameless One."

The Shazan has everyone focus on the centerpiece, a holographic representation of a blazing fire, and then leads the group in a chant that sounds oddly familiar, as if I've heard it in a dream.

After several minutes, the chanting comes to a close and everyone meditates in silence. Then the Shazan moves clockwise within the circle, administering the

Anosh to each person in turn. The drug is in the shape of a milky-white, paper-thin wafer the size of a dime, and all are instructed to let it sit on the tongue until it dissolves.

I observe Lunaria receive a wafer on her tongue and then close her mouth, smiling. The Shazan kneels in front of me, and I'm just about to tell her that I will be abstaining, when I make eye contact and am startled by her gaze—deeply intimate and yet impersonal, both down-to-earth and other-worldly. Without any sort of conscious thought process, I find myself opening my mouth and sticking out my tongue, accepting the wafer with a mixture of curiosity and dread.

The Shazan moves on to the woman on my left, and I close my mouth and feel the Anosh dissolve on my tongue, leaving a faint bitter taste, similar to hops. I'm wondering how long it will be before I feel the effects, when Lunaria, as if reading my mind, leans over and whispers in my ear, "It takes about ten minutes for the Anosh to kick in."

When it does, the first thing I experience is a wave of nausea, as if I were in a small craft on a stormy sea. I glance at Lunaria, who is doubled over with the dry heaves and looks as queasy as I feel.

"Do not fear the negative emotions that may arise," says the Shazan. "We all carry around much crap. You must wade through your shit before you reach the other shore."

My mind starts to race as the nausea subsides, and although my mission is to look after Lunaria, it becomes increasingly difficult to focus on anything other than what I'm experiencing internally, which is highly unpleasant, centering on feelings of desolation. With eyes closed, I sense that my body has grown colossal, as if I am a giant towering over my surroundings. Other people are tiny insects, scurrying around with no apparent purpose, so removed from me that I have no feelings toward them whatsoever.

Within I am empty—a husk of a man, a vacant fortress entirely devoid of life, a frozen wilderness in which nothing stirs except a bitter wind.

Other participants cry and moan. The woman on my left is whimpering like an injured pup, and when I open my eyes to look at her, for a moment I'm convinced that it's Angelica, returned from the grave. My heart overflows with love for my wife. Hope stirs within me for the first time since I tried to drown myself. But as I look at her, I realize that it's merely a strong resemblance—that this woman is a stranger, my Angelica is gone forever—and I am plunged back into despair, cut off from all human warmth. Alone, so alone in the world.

Unable to remain upright any longer, I lie down on the floor with my head on the cushion, and my body sinks through the floor, drops through the entire building and into the earth, tunneling into it like a neutrino, right through the molten core and out the other side of the planet, falling through space until I'm suspended in an inky void.

As if from a great distance, I hear Lunaria's voice. Although her words are pure gibberish, I can sense their tone, which is one of apprehension. She's worried about me. But when I try to reassure her, I find I am unable to speak, producing instead a sickly bellow, like that of a dying moose.

I get a strong whiff of urine and realize I have wet myself. It dawns on me that the overpowering emotion I'm experiencing is terror. My body trembles, my mind floods with anxiety, and I am left to steep in misery, wishing to hell I'd never taken the Anosh, wondering if I will ever return to normal, and fearing that I have done permanent damage to my brain.

And now I sense my body being stretched in all directions, like I'm being drawn and quartered. My muscles are extended to the breaking point—cartilage tearing, tendons and ligaments snapping, bones fracturing, joints bursting—the pain unimaginable—utterly unbearable, and still I must bear it, over a span of time that seems endless.

I grow convinced that what is happening to me is not random or haphazard, that a malicious entity is inflicting this horrendous pain on me. Instantly I become aware of a gruff male voice taunting me and laughing sadistically, taking great delight in my suffering.

I hear myself screaming, the tortured sounds echoing through the void. And again, from a vast distance, seemingly from another dimension altogether, I hear a voice. This time it's the Shazan, who makes as if to calm me down, to comfort me. Again, most of it comes across as gobbledygook, but there's one statement I comprehend: I should listen to the voice of Incognolio.

Between the thunderous sadistic laughter and my own echoing screams, I am gradually able to make out the remote sound of a female voice. Sweet and inviting, singing the most soothing, mellifluous song I've ever heard, it is the voice that spoke to me while I was on the verge of drowning. The more I focus on it, the louder it grows, eclipsing and finally silencing the vicious laughter, and in so doing, the voice of Incognolio eradicates all of my pain.

What follows feels like coming home. My original home, like an infant suckling at its mother's breast. Sheer ecstasy, surrounded by boundless love, basking in the affection of an all-embracing, all-accepting deity whose light illuminates my mind, whose compassion liberates my soul, whose song entices me to let go of my fears, surrender my self until all boundaries dissolve and I am merged with the Goddess.

Only I can't.

As delightful as it feels, and as much as I'd like to fully submit, a part of me resists. Perhaps out of instinct, perhaps out of some perverse need to oppose, or perhaps out of loyalty to my unflagging sense of worthlessness, the unshakeable conviction that at the core I remain unlovable.

And in this moment, in which I falter and begin to pull away, all is lost. I plunge from the rapturous heights of Incognolio, her voice receding into the muffled background, and plummet head-first back into the darkness, the agony, the relentless pain, all the while being ridiculed and debased by that vicious, sadistic bastard whom I now recognize as Mazazel.

CHAPTER TWENTY-NINE

DOCTOR DJINN

I awaken to excruciating pain, and when I open my eyes I find myself lying on a sofa in a strange place I've never seen before. I manage to stand up and walk around—wincing with each step—and stumble into the bathroom, where steam rises from behind the shower curtain.

I take a piss, a burning sensation coursing through my penis, and when I flush the toilet, Lunaria calls out, "Misha, is that you?" I answer in the affirmative. She shuts off the water and pulls the curtain aside, revealing her naked body in all its glory. I turn away from her and, as she towels off, ask how I have come to be at her apartment.

Donning a bathrobe, Lunaria explains that I fell asleep toward the end of the ceremony, and when dawn arrived and the Shazan sounded the gong, one of the participants helped Lunaria carry me to his car. He drove the two of us to Lunaria's apartment and helped carry me upstairs and onto the sofa, where I continued to sleep for several hours while she dozed in her bed.

She asks whether I'd like to take a shower, but I decline, worried that the spray of water will feel like needles piercing my battered body. But since my pants reek of urine, I accept her offer of a fresh set of clothes, courtesy of a former boyfriend.

As Lunaria cooks breakfast, I ask her how long it will take for the Anosh to wear off, and she replies that the effects should already have dissipated. But I insist that I am still tripping, having awakened in tremendous pain, my body and mind feeling shattered, like I'm living in hell. Not to mention—indeed, I keep this to myself— that I can still hear the cackle and snort of Mazazel.

Lunaria comes over and strokes my hair, looks down at me with pity and compassion, and explains that in rare cases Anosh has been known to produce a prolonged effect, at times extending to several weeks. This apparently happened to her one time, although it was altogether different, since she was stuck not in hell, but in heaven, where she walked around in a perpetual state of euphoria.

This comes as bad news indeed, since I can't imagine how I'll make it through the next *hour*, let alone the next several weeks. And now I have no appetite, so

I simply sit across from her while Lunaria eats her eggs and grackle. She tells me that she hadn't realized until last night, when I was crying and grieving during the Wakan, that Angelica had died.

"I'm so sorry for your loss," she says. "But on the bright side, this means that the two of us can be together."

"Afraid not," I reply. "You know that I can't have an intimate relationship with a patient, Lunnie. Even a former patient."

"That's a stupid rule. What if the two of you are in love?"

"There's no exception for love. It's a violation of professional boundaries, a breach of trust. Like with a parent and child. There's an imbalance of power inherent in the therapist-patient relationship that doesn't vanish simply because the treatment ends."

"Why, that's just a bunch of words!" Lunaria bangs the table with her fist. "The two of us would be great together!"

I shake my head. "Lunaria, you don't even know the real me. As your therapist, I always focused on *your* needs. In real life I'm not nearly so selfless."

"Big fucking deal. I'm *used* to boyfriends who are assholes."

She then smiles beguilingly, and I find myself imagining going to her and lifting her to her feet, kissing those swollen lips, running my hands under the robe, cupping her breast with one hand as I caress her shapely tush with the other, then sweeping her up into my arms, whisking her into the bedroom, and making passionate love to her for hours on end.

Mazazel bursts out laughing. I shake myself out of my reverie, and then I spend the next half-hour fending off arguments from Lunaria as to why the prohibition against sex with former patients is unfair, outdated, and patently absurd. Each time I counter her line of reasoning she becomes increasingly agitated, so I say the matter is closed and she stomps off to her bedroom to get dressed. I feel like it's time to leave, but I sense that a goodbye hug from Lunaria could undermine my self-restraint, so I write a quick thank-you note on a napkin and slip out the front door.

Out on the street, I pass a bank with a digital clock reading 3:45, which startles me, having forgotten how late I went to sleep. I'm forced to take a taxi to get to my therapy appointment on time, arriving just as Dr. Djinn is opening his office door.

I sit down across from him and, after describing my experiences at the Wakan, say that I don't know whether to laugh or cry at the horror of existence.

"Doctor, I'm living in a state of physical, mental, emotional, and spiritual torment. I'm taunted by the cruel and pitiless voice of Mazazel, who mocks and denigrates me."

"I see," says Dr. Djinn. "And does this Mazazel remind you of anyone in particular?"

The answer jumps right out at me, and I think it strange that the connection hadn't occurred to me earlier.

"There are definite parallels to my father," I say. "Not that he was demonic, of course. But when I was young, he loomed over me as a massive and terrifying figure. During his worst moods, he was vicious and traumatizing, engaging in both physical and emotional abuse.

"Even during lighter moments when we played together, he seemed to forget how much bigger and stronger he was. My father loved to pin me down and tickle me, taking great delight in my squeals and laughter. He was oblivious to the fact that I was screaming to be released from what amounted to torture, the experience of utter helplessness in the face of being violated. Something akin to rape."

"Yes." Dr. Djinn nods. "And this Incognolio could represent aspects of your mother, who nurtured you. She surrounded you with love and acceptance, providing experiences of soothing and comfort, of ecstatic merging. Which on some level you perceived as seductive and you ultimately rejected, leaving you even more exposed to the dangers of your father's sadism."

"This all makes sense," I reply, "but I'm wary of viewing Incognolio and Mazazel purely as projections of early feelings toward my parents. I experienced them during the Wakan as all-too-real entities, and even at this very moment I hear the fiendish voice of Mazazel and feel that he subjects me to intolerable pain."

Dr. Djinn agrees. "These are not figments of your imagination, but powerful archetypes of the human un-conscious. Despite the emphasis on God-the-Father in Western religions, most cultures through the ages have associated the Female with a loving Goddess and the Male with a malicious, bestial Devil figure. This makes biological sense in that the infant's primary bond is gen-erally with the mother, who protects and cares for the child, whereas the father intrudes on this idyllic moth-er-child unit, and in time becomes the one who initiates the youngster into the harsh realities of the world. "*If*," the doctor adds, "he doesn't abandon mother and child altogether."

"That's all well and good," I say. "But no amount of intellectualizing can change the fact that I'm in trou-ble here—strung out on Anosh, terrorized by Mazazel, and facing the real possibility of several more weeks of this hell. Can't you prescribe some damn opiates or something? Without serious pain relief, I'm liable to kill myself."

"I'm not averse to using medications," Dr. Djinn replies. "But first I'd like to suggest another approach. A bold approach that could help resolve matters, although it would entail certain…risks."

Failing to imagine how things could possibly be any worse, I say I'm open to giving it a try, and Dr. Djinn nods and then asks me to please invite Mazazel to join the two of us in his office.

CHAPTER THIRTY

REPETITIVE
STRAIN INJURY

When the microwave beeps, I retrieve my heating pad, which is almost too hot to handle. I allow it to cool for a few seconds, and then wrap it around my right arm, which is in considerable pain due to RSI (repetitive strain injury) caused by the hours, days, and months I have spent typing my novel and manipulating the mouse.

At least that's what I told Shelly, the physical therapist, when she assessed my condition—and no doubt the long hours on the computer didn't help matters. But what I didn't mention to Shelly was that there was another factor. Ever since the deaths of Angelica and the twins I've been masturbating compulsively, sometimes two or three times a day—as a sexual release and a way of dealing with anxiety and depression, but also

as my only means of approximating the ecstatic dissolution of boundaries I experienced when I first heard
the voice of Incognolio.

In addition to the heating pad and the daily exercises Shelly prescribed, I am also trying to reduce the
strain on my arm by making use of voice recognition
software, which allows me to continue working on the
novel largely through dictation. Telling the story out
loud felt awkward at first, but I learned to do it with
my eyes shut, giving myself even greater access to the
subterranean depths of my unconscious.

With the shooting pains in my arm temporarily
soothed by the warmth of the heating pad, I return to
my desk, put on a headset microphone, and wonder
how in hell I'm going to personify Mazazel, whom I
vaguely conceptualize as the Dark Force or Lord of the
Underworld, and wishing to steer clear of stereotypical
portrayals of the Devil (a.k.a. Satan, Lucifer, Beelzebub,
Mephistopheles) involving horns, hooves, pointed tail,
trident, and so forth. Then I recall Voltaire's dictum and
decide to let readers visualize whatever they wish.

So, with a now familiar blend of curiosity and dread,
I go ahead and welcome Mazazel into Dr. Djinn's office.
There's a deafening roar, a blast of scorching heat, and a
nasty sulfuric stench—certain clichéd atmospherics being all but unavoidable—as Mazazel appears in one of
his countless material forms, perched on the oak desk.

This material manifestation of Mazazel is so un-
speakably grotesque, so monstrous, so hideous, that at
first I can only sneak quick glances at him before turning away, and it takes all of my courage not to flee from
the room in terror.

"I apologize for intruding upon your idyllic two-
some," says Mazazel mockingly, and then bursts out
laughing. "But after all, I *was* invited."

"Thank you for joining us," says Dr. Djinn. "There
appears to be considerable tension between you and
Misha, and I thought I might be able to provide a forum
for resolving your differences."

"By all means!" Mazazel chuckles. "Fire away!"

"First of all," I say, "could you please give me a break
and dial down the torment, so I can at least hear myself
think?"

"Consider it done," says Mazazel, and for the first
time since I left the loving embrace of the Goddess Incognolio, I am free of pain.

"Thank you." I heave a huge sigh of relief. "Now, I'd
like to know what the hell I did to deserve such punishment."

"Let me remind you," says Mazazel, "that you were
free to remain merged with that pathetic harlot, Incognolio. You *chose* to leave her, to separate yourself, and
separation inevitably brings suffering."

"Fair enough. But why so much?"

"Look, I have nothing against you personally," says Mazazel. "You seem like a decent enough chap. It's simply my job to inflict misery and destruction upon the human race. You see, I am the Yang to Incognolio's Yin. Without this duality, there would be no world at all."

This actually makes sense, and I am taken aback, having failed to anticipate that the brutish miscreant would turn out to be so articulate.

"Okay," I say, "but why would an impersonal force take such great delight in bringing harm? In other words, why are you such a sadistic bastard?"

Mazazel grins, exposing his hideous teeth.

"Simple. Because you humans have that which I lack—free will. And I despise you mongrels for it."

"You've gotta be kidding! So it's because you're *jealous*? That's it?"

Mazazel fumes, but remains silent.

"That's mighty small of you," I say. "And I'll bet you're jealous of Incognolio as well, since *she* inspires worship and adoration while you elicit nothing but fear, hatred, and scorn."

Smoke pours out of Mazazel's ears, and once again I am racked with pain.

"You have the emotional maturity of a three-year-old," I say. "No wonder the world's so fucked up!"

My pain level skyrockets, until I'm in even greater agony than before.

"This hasn't helped at all," I say, turning to Dr. Djinn.

"Ah, what a shame," Dr. Djinn replies, and to my horror, he slowly morphs into a demon every bit as repulsive as Mazazel. "If this was not beneficial, perhaps you would prefer a lobotomy. I'd be happy to perform it myself right now."

Dr. Djinn laughs diabolically as a collection of gleaming instruments of torture materializes on his desk, and I run screaming from his office.

CHAPTER THIRTY-ONE

THE MEDICAL ARTS & CRAFTS BUILDING

Now I'm sprinting down the street in such unimaginable distress that all I can think about is how to end the pain—I'll do anything to stop it—and the first thing that springs to mind is suicide.

I don't own a gun or have access to poison, so I figure the quickest and easiest way would be to jump off a building. The tallest building is Dork Tower, which has been true in every city in the country ever since President Dork decreed that no building can rise higher than the ones he owns and had all taller skyscrapers demolished. But I'll be damned if I will even set foot in an edifice named for that schmuck, so I head for the Medical Arts & Crafts Building, just ten blocks away.

As I dash full speed down the sidewalk, dodging pedestrians, dogs, and pooshka vendors, I think that if only I hadn't run into Lunaria I wouldn't have attended the Wakan, in which case I wouldn't have ingested the Anosh and had my fateful encounter with Mazazel. But then again, even before the Wakan I was pretty depressed and hopeless, so in truth, either way probably would have ended with me taking my own life.

As I approach the Medical Arts & Crafts Building, huffing and puffing, I am surprised to see my twin brother, Laszlo Skuntch, approaching from the opposite direction, and when he spots me he starts running, too.

We meet in front of the building, and Laszlo, who is carrying a shopping bag from Schmenken's, asks me what I'm doing.

"I'm in so much goddamn pain," I say. "I'm going to jump off the top of the MA&C."

"That's unacceptable!" Laszlo replies, grabbing my arm. "My novel, *Mazazel*, isn't about a suicide. It's about a man who *murders* his twin brother."

I try to shake him off, but his grip is so secure that I might as well be trying to shake off my own arm. "Fine, Laszlo, you can push me off of the damn building."

"I've used that method in a previous novel, and I never use the same method twice. We'll have to come up with another plan, and you'll have to try to escape from me, Misha, since it spoils all the fun if my victim *wants* to die."

"Fuck you, Laszlo," I say. "I'm not a character in your stupid novel. I'm a character in *Incognolio*, which *I'm* writing, and I say it's going to be a goddamn suicide. So piss off and find yourself another fucking victim. Perhaps we were triplets separated at birth and on your way home you can run into your *other* brother."

"Far too contrived. I'm going to stick with killing you, so you'd better start fleeing. I've never used suffocation before, and I happen to have this Schmenken's bag, which will do nicely." Laszlo pulls a new pair of trousers out of the bag and tosses them aside.

After my horrific near-drowning experience, I have no interest in being suffocated, so I kick Laszlo in the groin. He falls to the ground, and I run into the Medical Arts & Crafts building and make a beeline for the elevators, quickly pressing the up button.

It seems to take forever for an elevator to reach the lobby, and by the time I'm inside, Laszlo is racing toward me. I hit the button for the 20th floor and the doors slide closed just in the nick of time.

Up I go, to the retreating sound of Laszlo's cursing. When I reach the top floor, a bell sounds and I scoot out of there. Hanging a left, I tear down the hall, searching for a way up to the roof. I turn a corner and am halfway down the corridor when I spot what I'm looking for.

It's a heavy black door marked *Egress*. But the fucking thing's locked, and now I'm screwed because I already hear Laszlo's footsteps approaching.

Between my thwarted plan for suicide and the unbearable pain, a part of me just wants to surrender to my brother and let him put me out of my misery. But another part of me rejects this idea on principle. Plus, I'd love to fuck up his writerly aspirations. So when he appears, I run right at the bastard and easily tackle him, having played linebacker for my varsity football team. Now the two of us are wrestling on the ground, a pretty even match since we are identical twins. But I manage to straddle him and beat his face to a pulp, knocking him unconscious with one final jab to the temple.

I skedaddle via elevator, and on the way down it occurs to me that if Laszlo used this elevator to enter *my* universe, perhaps I can use it to slip into an alternate one. This may or may not put me out of Mazazel's reach, but it seems well worth a try.

I hit the button for the sixth floor, but when the doors open the carpet is still blue. I return to the lobby, then head back up to the sixth floor. Still nothing has changed, so it's back down to the lobby. When the doors open this time, there's Laszlo, bloody-faced and grinning, and I punch the button for the sixth floor. But before the doors close, Laszlo squeezes through and pounces on me.

A brutal fight ensues—flying fists and vicious karate kicks to the chest and head. Meanwhile, each time the elevator reaches the sixth floor I glance at the carpet, which remains blue, then hit the button for the lobby. After several trips up and down, Laszlo manages to knock me to the floor—face down—and straddle my body. Then he grabs the Schmenken's bag and slips it over my head, pulling the drawstring tight against my neck.

"This is fantastic!" he gloats. "It's my first murder-in-an-elevator scene."

"Fuck you, asshole." I gasp for air. "*I'm* writing this scene and it doesn't end with my goddamn death."

But it doesn't look good: I'm all out of air and slowly passing out. When the bell sounds for the lobby, it takes all my remaining strength to inch my fingers up to the control panel, fumble around until I've located the right button, and press it.

The doors close. My arm falls back to the floor. As I feel the elevator car ascend, my entire life flashes before my eyes, heralding the end. The elevator bell sounds one last time, and just before I black out I hear a voice shout, "What the *fuck*?"

CHAPTER THIRTY-TWO

UNIVERSE-HOPPING

On something of a roll, and feeling pleased with how the last few chapters jelled, I eagerly set out on the next one. But I soon find that I have no idea how to proceed. I'm intimidated by the prospect of having to choose which among the infinite number of possible alternate universes to drop Misha and Laszlo into, of choosing just *one* out of that seething multitude.

I remind myself not to overthink it, to simply let the story go where it needs to go. But that's far easier said than done, and I'm becoming increasingly discouraged when Yiddle squawks, *Mystical arts! Mystical arts!* Which reminds me that I've got to get to the first meeting of my class in Universe-Hopping. I throw on a jacket, head downstairs, and turn left on Random Road toward Circle Square.

As I stroll down the sidewalk, I come clean and admit to the reader that I—Muldoon—have been writing this story all along. That I invented Paige's beachside bungalow where Micaela supposedly worked on *Incognolio*, as well as Misha, the grieving father of stillborn twins, and Laszlo, Misha's evil twin brother who is writing *Mazazel*—all of it fabricated from whole cloth, designed to lure the reader into yet another narrative that feigns authenticity, only to prove fictitious in the end.

Why I get such a kick out of this authorial sleight of hand is anybody's guess. Perhaps I've felt deceived and betrayed so many times over the course of my life that there's a certain satisfaction to be gained in turning the tables on others. Or maybe the shattering of fictional worlds represents my attempt to question the nature of reality and to confront mortality, much as Paige proclaimed in her writers' group.

Whatever my reasons, I'm tired of playing the trickster, and I sense that this tale is nearing its end, although I haven't a clue how to wrap it up, which is distressing because there's nothing worse than a good yarn that ends on a false note.

But having relied on the wisdom—and perversity—of my subconscious mind all along, there's no reason to change horses now, so I set aside worrying about the ending and instead arrive at Circle Square, enter the

Mystical Arts Building, take the elevator up to the sixth floor, and locate room 639.

A few minutes later, when everyone has arrived—ten in all—the instructor, a cute pixie-like woman in her late twenties, introduces herself as Deedle and welcomes everyone to the wonderful world of universe-hopping.

Deedle has everyone in the circle introduce themselves and tell a little about what drew them to this topic. When it's my turn, I say that my name is Muldoon, and that while high on Ink, I traveled to an alternate universe in which my twin sister, Micaela, survived birth and grew up to be my best friend. I leave out the part about being lovers.

"When the drug wore off and I awoke back home, I felt lonelier than ever and longed to be reunited with my sister. I continued to ingest Ink at every opportunity, but each time I took it, I ended up in a different universe. Some of them were nightmarish, and none of them contained Micaela, so I was excited when I happened to see an infomercial about this class on late night cable TV."

When everyone has shared their stories, Deedle tells her own story of how she was on a honeymoon cruise with Dunkin, the love of her life. One morning, Dunkin was attending a private lesson with the cruise ship's tennis pro, when the pro smashed a high-velocity shot straight into Dunkin's balls, causing him to faint, collapse to the ground, crack his skull, and die on the spot.

Condolences are expressed, and Deedle continues, "I was so overwhelmed with sorrow that I landed in a psychiatric ward, where a psychologist told me about Elisabeth Kubler-Ross's five stages of grief—denial, anger, bargaining, depression, and acceptance. But I felt I could never accept the loss of my soul mate, and after the hospital released me, I began consulting with mediums who claimed to put people in touch with the deceased.

"Well, they all turned out to be frauds," says Deedle. "I was ready to give up on that approach when I heard about Cecil Vernax, a renowned medium who was said to have helped Yoko Ono contact John Lennon. I consulted with Cecil at his home office, and he turned out to be the real deal. I was actually able to speak with Dunkin, who told me that he wasn't dead, that he was living in an alternate universe where the tennis pro had cancelled his lesson that day. He said the honeymoon was a smashing success, and we were living in wedded bliss.

"I was ecstatic. I asked Dunkin to describe each and every detail of the universe he lives in, vowing to find a way to join him as soon as I learned how to universe-hop.

"Afterwards, I went straight to the library and took out every book I could find on quantum mechanics. Modern physicists have theorized what the ancient seers knew intuitively: that an infinite number of alternate universes coexist. According to the Many-Worlds Interpretation of quantum mechanics, there are many other worlds, similar to this one, which exist in parallel at the same space and time. In fact, every time an event takes place, the universe splits between the various options available. Everything that *can* happen *does* happen. Instead of the one continuous timeline we typically imagine, the universe looks more like a series of branches splitting off of a tree trunk.

"For example," says Deedle as she turns to me, "there's a universe where Muldoon won the lottery last night and decided to skip this class. And another where he came down with pneumonia, or was hit by a bus on his way here and died."

I'm struck by this revelation, mind-boggled to think about all those alternate Muldoons. And oddly reassured, too, because with so many other selves out there, so many other lives I'm living and deaths I'm dying, whatever happens to me in this universe doesn't seem so important.

"I went online and discovered that courses on Quantum Jumping were all the rage," Deedle is saying. "They promised that I could pop into parallel dimensions and acquire creativity, wisdom, skills, and inspiration from alternate versions of myself. I forked over a bundle to gain access to these esoteric teachings. Some of these guys suggested using your imagination to create a bridge to other universes, like a handshake across time and space. Others referred to thought transference and changing the frequency of your thinking, like tuning into a different radio station. One even suggested that in order to make the jump to an alternate universe you had to enter into a state of mind in which you forget everything you know about *this* universe.

"But it all amounted to a hill of garbanzos, and I felt I was back at square one. So I went to see Cecil again and asked him if he'd had other clients whose loved ones turned out to be in alternate universes rather than deceased. And he said there had been several dozen, and when I asked him if there were any commonalities in these cases, he replied that in each case the person had been violently killed in their home universe, but survived in the alternate."

Deedle smiles, her face simply radiant.

"That's how I came upon my method for universe-hopping. You could call it high-risk, I suppose. But unlike all the online courses, this technique actually works.

"The idea is to find out everything you possibly can about your target universe until you can clearly visualize it. Then, while you are concentrating with all your might on your universe of choice, arrange to be violently killed."

Muttering and sighs of dismay arise from the students, who think Deedle's gone bonkers. But she's prepared for such a reaction.

"I know I'm offering a radical technique, and I wouldn't expect anyone to try it without concrete evidence that it works." At this point, Deedle walks over to a door that leads to the next classroom, opens the door, and gestures to someone inside the adjoining room. It's a tall, ruggedly handsome young man who enters the classroom and waves to everyone, smiling, and Deedle says, "I'd like to introduce you all to Dunkin."

Everyone gasps, and I am truly impressed.

Following a hushed silence, Deedle explains that we're all living in the alternate universe in which the cruise ship's tennis pro cancelled Dunkin's lesson and Dunkin wasn't killed by a ball to the nuts. Deedle threw herself in front of an oncoming subway car while visualizing this universe, and successfully accomplished the hop.

Now doubt creeps in, and I ask, "How do we know that you didn't make up the whole story about Dunkin being killed?"

Deedle is prepared for this objection as well.

"On the day that I made the hop, I purposely brought along a memento of my home universe."

Deedle grins as she retrieves a folded page of newsprint from her pocket, unfolds it, and holds up for all to see the front page of *The Informer* from November 9th of the previous year, whose headline reveals that Rod Shaft—not Peter Pecker, as in my universe—won the presidential election. This is nothing less than remarkable, and everyone is on their feet giving Deedle a standing ovation.

When the class breaks up, I'm walking down the hall thinking up ways to violently kill myself. As I arrive at the elevator, the bell rings and the doors slide open to reveal Laszlo straddling Misha, holding a Schmenken's plastic bag tightly over his head. "What the *fuck?*" I exclaim.

CHAPTER THIRTY-THREE

FULL OF SHIT

Having been unable to settle on an alternate universe into which I'd transport Misha and Laszlo, I left it up to my subconscious mind, which apparently landed them smack dab in my own universe, literally right under my nose.

This development is bound to complicate matters—as if the manuscript weren't already convoluted enough—but I can't just stand there watching as my father is murdered by my uncle, so I set out to rescue Misha. I push the elevator's emergency-stop button, throw Laszlo off of Misha, and—just in the nick of time—remove the Schmenken's bag from my father's head.

Laszlo attacks, forcing me to deliver a swift, vicious kick to his groin so he'll stay down. Misha responds to mouth-to-mouth resuscitation, and after a brief coughing fit, the first thing he does is comment excitedly that the carpeting in the hallway is green.

"I'm free of that bastard!" he shouts, no doubt referring to Mazazel.

"Relax, Misha," I say. "No one will harm you now. Mazazel and Laszlo—as well as you yourself—are all characters in the novel I'm writing, titled *Incognolio*. And I don't plan on extending your section of the story, seeing as it's pretty much played out."

This little speech of mine elicits derisive laughter from both Misha, who maintains that *he* is writing *Incognolio*, and Laszlo, who insists that this is actually a scene from his novel, *Mazazel*.

"I still fully intend to kill Misha," Laszlo adds, gingerly adjusting his rod and tackle, "after which Mazazel will be free to torment him throughout the endless reaches of eternity."

This is all very confusing, and I propose that the three of us go out for a drink, to which they agree. We take the elevator down to the lobby and head across the street to my favorite watering hole, Hrabal's Tavern.

"Good to see you, Muldoon," says Hrabal. He seats our small group at a table and serves each of us a Jack Daniels on the rocks.

"Look, you guys," I say. "You're no longer in Misha's home universe, where you are both authors and Laszlo is set on murdering his twin brother. So why not get with the program and accept that in this particular universe, you are merely characters in my novel."

"Screw you, buddy," replies Laszlo. "I'm not *merely* anything anywhere, and I don't give two shits about your bogus novel. I'm still composing *Mazazel* at this very moment. So, unless you'd like to be rubbed out as well, Muldoon, you can go take a flying fuck at a rolling donut."

"I'm afraid you're both mistaken," says Misha. "I've been writing *Incognolio* ever since I nearly drowned myself. I invented Laszlo, my homicidal twin brother, in order to introduce an element of danger to the story. And you—Muldoon—are my original protagonist, an extrapolation of how my real son might have turned out had he lived."

This discussion is not going as well as I'd hoped, and just as I set out to prove that I am indeed the legitimate author of the story, my chair collapses under me and I crash to the floor.

"Ha!" shouts Laszlo. "And I suppose you pulled this stunt for comic relief?"

This sounds plausible and I'm about to confirm his hunch when a pigeon flies into the tavern, circles the room, and proceeds to take an enormous dump directly on my head, the white gunk soiling my hair and drizzling down my face.

Everyone in the bar is having a good laugh at my expense, as Laszlo stands and then bows repeatedly, taking full credit for my plight.

But Misha is not so easily convinced. When Laszlo sits back down, Misha turns to him and says, "If you were truly writing this story, Laszlo, then you would have strangled me to death on the elevator. But the fact is that *I'm* in control of the narrative and therefore I had Muldoon rescue me."

To prove his point, Misha claps his hands and his brother's chair collapses. There's another round of laughter as Laszlo crashes to the floor. Then a labradoodle wanders into the bar, makes a beeline for Laszlo, lifts his leg, and soaks him with urine from head to toe.

Sputtering with anger and humiliation, Laszlo claps *his* hands, and Misha plummets to the ground, his chair having gone the way of the others. Before he knows what hit him, a rotund fellow sitting at the next table clutches his belly, turns, and pukes all over Misha, inundating him with a seemingly endless cascade of yellowish chunk-filled vomit.

Now the three of us are sprawled out on the floor, each one drenched in repulsive excretions. The odor of poop, piss, and puke wafts through the tavern, while the other patrons point and convulse with laughter. I'm about to retreat to my study with my tail between my legs, maybe have a cup of joe and try to figure out how to redeem such a ludicrous scene, when who should appear but Pizza Guy. He pulls me to my feet, proffering a bar towel with which to wipe myself off, and leads me to a booth in the corner, where Hrabal brings a Jack Daniels for me and a White Russian for Pizza Guy.

"The joke's on you, Muldoon," says Pizza Guy, my pal who claims to be completing a degree in philosophy from Imaginary University. "Did you get the message?"

"Huh? What message?"

"Each scene carries a message, like in a dream. This last one spoke loud and clear: You're full of shit."

"No kidding," I say, wiping the pigeon poop from my face and hair. "And why exactly is that?"

"Because you persist in believing that you're in control of the narrative."

"Let me assure you that I *am* writing the damn thing, despite what those two clowns say." I gesture toward Misha and Laszlo, who continue to amuse the crowd with their antics.

"What proof do we have of that, Muldoon? Because you periodically adjourn to your study, where you sit at your desk and purportedly type this manuscript? But how is *that* Muldoon any less fictional than the one I'm currently addressing?"

I'm silent, since this enigma has in fact been bothering me all along.

"Let's say Author Muldoon gets hungry, stops typing, and orders a pizza," says Pizza Guy. "Is the pizza guy who shows up at his door more real than I am, sitting here talking to Protagonist Muldoon?"

"No, I suppose not."

"Then how is Author Muldoon any less fictional than Protagonist Muldoon?"

"But *someone* must be doing the writing! It can't write itself, for Christ's sake."

"But it can!" exclaims Pizza Guy, his eyes ablaze. "Let's suppose that both of us are characters in a story being written by a novelist whom we'll call...say, Sussman."

"Why Sussman?"

"First name that popped into my head. Now, the question arises: Is Sussman controlling the narrative?"

"If he's the author, then by definition he's in control."

"Ah, but by *whose* definition?" asks Pizza Guy. "If you're using the traditional definition—the Romantic notion of the author as solitary creator—then I agree with your conclusion. But what if authorship is a social construct that's obsolete? What if the meaning of a text lies not in its rendition but in its interpretation by the reader? And what if the very self is a construct, with no inherent reality? Then this Sussman is as much of a phantasm as we are!"

"Okaaay," I say. "So you're saying the narrative basically writes itself?"

"That's one way of putting it," Pizza Guy replies. "Another is to say that it already resides in Incognolio."

"Incognolio?"

"Yes, the Realm of Imagination. It's the source of everything that exists, fictional or otherwise."

This comes as a revelation. Can it be that Pizza Guy has just bestowed upon me the answer to my quest?

"You once said that you're at one with Incognolio," I remind him. "How exactly did you accomplish that?"

"Come with me, Muldoon, and I'll show you."

CHAPTER THIRTY-FOUR

REALM OF IMAGINATION

When I get up to leave, Pizza Guy shakes his head and has me sit back down.

"You only need to close your eyes to cross the threshold," he says. "Incognolio lies within."

Somehow this sounds scarier than traveling to an actual place. I ask him to tell me more about the Realm of Imagination.

"Unlike the dimension we live in," he explains, "it's a timeless realm unbounded by rationality. It's the creative source of ideas and inventions, as well as the dream world and the artistic imagination. Fairy tales and myths, psychedelic and mystical experiences all derive from this domain. It's the realm of Psyche or Soul, and of the Archetypes, intersecting with human imagination and yet infinitely more vast, encompassing the

Astral Plane, the Land of the Gods, and Cosmic Consciousness."

This description doesn't put me at ease. In fact, it
intensifies my anxiety. But when I express reservations
about making the trip on my own, Pizza Guy says, "Relax, Muldoon, I'll be at your side the whole time."

I experience yet again that now familiar blend of
dread and curiosity. But there's something so reassur-
ing about the sound of Pizza Guy's voice, something so
heartening about his sweet, guileless disposition, that I
feel confident in placing my trust in him.

Before I can close my eyes, though, I must first ask a
question that's been hounding me.

"How can I—Protagonist Muldoon—enter Incognolio if that means fully surrendering the notion that I'm
in control of the narrative, when I know full well that as
Author Muldoon, I'm still typing away at my computer
keyboard?"

"I thought we were past that," says Pizza Guy. "I
thought you agreed that Author Muldoon is no less fictional than Protagonist Muldoon. But I tell you what. If
it'll ease your mind and aid your entry into Incognolio,
I suggest that we reunite in Author Muldoon's world by
having him take a break from writing and order a pizza,
which I'll promptly deliver."

I feel a little silly making such a request, especially
this late in the game, but what the hell. So I stop typing,

pick up the phone, and place an order for a large pizza. Since I happen to know that Pizza Guy is vegetarian, I ask for a cheese pizza with spinach on one half and Italian sausage on the other.

Yiddle had been flying in and out of my study, and as I hang up the phone, she lands on my desk. Looking up at me intently, she squawks, *Polly want a cracker*! I know she's being ironic, but I fetch her one anyway.

After she's eaten the cracker she asks, *Who writes our dialogue when you're not typing*?

"I suppose it's this Sussman fellow," I reply. "But I wouldn't worry your feathered little head about it, Yiddle. According to Pizza Guy he's nothing special, since the so-called real world is just as ephemeral as this fictional one. In fact, Pizza Guy—who's only a couple of credits shy of a doctorate in philosophy, mind you—claims that the physical world appears to have been derived from mathematical equations. So it seems that *everything* originates from the Realm of Imagination, into which he shall usher me momentarily."

When the doorbell rings, Yiddle squawks, *Danger*! *Danger*! This takes me by surprise, since I trust Pizza Guy implicitly. I figure perhaps this is one of those rare occasions when Yiddle is actually mistaken. However, when I go downstairs and open the door, it isn't Pizza Guy—it's my villainous uncle, Laszlo Skuntch, with his fiendish eyes, pencil-thin mustache, and stupid black beret.

"What the hell are *you* doing here?" I ask the jerk, who still reeks of dog piss.

"Hah!" he replies. "Thought you could get rid of me by leaving your little subplot unresolved?"

"Where's Pizza Guy?" I inquire, although I already know the answer.

"Let's just say that he's delivered his last pie." Laszlo beams triumphantly, and I want to punch him in his fucking face.

To be honest, I have mixed feelings about this turn of events. On the one hand, I am going to miss Pizza Guy and I'm disappointed because now I'll probably never figure out how to gain entry to the Realm of Imagination. On the other, it feels good to be relieved of the daunting task of rendering a description of that Realm.

"I suppose you murdered Misha, too?" I ask.

"Of course." Laszlo laughs maniacally. "You see, I've decided that by the end of my novel I will have knocked off every damn character in the story."

"Why?"

"Because I can."

"Killing people gives you a sense of power?" I ask. "Perhaps you need to explore why you feel so impotent."

"What are you, my fucking therapist?"

"For instance, maybe as a child you had an unempathic caretaker and internalized a sense of inadequacy."

"Nice try, Muldoon, but I'm afraid you're attributing to me a depth of character that doesn't exist. I'm the Evil Twin Brother, the Psychopathic Crime Novelist, case closed."

Laszlo's right. Like so many of my characters, I never really took the time to give him a coherent backstory, so he remains two-dimensional, lacking the complexities associated with real psychological depth.

Furthermore, although I'm capable of assigning flaws to my good characters, my bad ones—whether it's Laszlo, ghostwriter Dick Fracken, Micaela's husband Jack, or Mazazel—are purely evil, devoid of any redeeming characteristics.

This observation supports what my therapist, Dr. Miranda, has been telling me all along, that I have difficulty integrating good and bad within myself, and tend to project evil onto others.

Having gained this new insight, I'm determined to humanize Laszlo and demonstrate that he's capable of compassion, so I invite him upstairs for pizza.

But as soon as Laszlo enters the apartment, he runs after Yiddle, chasing her from room to room and heaping verbal abuse upon my sweet bird. I try to tackle

Laszlo, but he eludes my grasp, and I end up lying on the floor of my study, watching helplessly as my uncle lunges and captures my pet. Yiddle squawks pathetically as Laszlo grasps her by the neck, lifts her over his head, and swings the poor creature around in a circle until her neck snaps.

"You fucking asshole!" I cry, getting up off the floor and pouncing on Laszlo. "I'll kill you, you motherfucker!"

Enraged by the loss of Pizza Guy, Misha, and now Yiddle, I drag Laszlo to the ground and sit on top of him, pounding away mercilessly at his face with my fists. Just when I think he's done for, Laszlo lifts his legs, wraps his ankles around my neck, and jerks me backward. Before I know it, he's sitting on top of me, grinning maliciously, his knees pinning my arms to the floor. With blood streaming down his face from multiple wounds, Laszlo reaches over to my desk and grabs my mouse, and then loops the cord around my neck.

"Fancy yourself a writer, eh?" he says. "Well, let's see how you do at describing your own death throes!"

With my arms pinned, there's nothing I can do to prevent him from tightening the cord. I try lifting my legs, but I'm not quite agile enough to replicate Laszlo's move. As my heart pounds and I grow lightheaded, it occurs to me that this is *precisely* what I want—the opportunity to universe-hop via violent death—so I focus my consciousness on the alternate universe in which I live with Micaela.

I picture her lovely face, our shared bedroom, Yiddle the German Shepherd, the sofa seemingly made of cheese, the luscious Vernulian food, the bookstore named Title Wave, my Pulitzer Prize-winning novel selling like chowcakes. And then, returning to the image of my beloved, smiling sister, I expire.

CHAPTER THIRTY-FIVE

THE OL' SWITCHEROO

The transition to my new universe is quick and painless, and when I open my eyes to the loving gaze of my twin sister, I feel immensely grateful to Deedle for having shared such an extraordinary discovery.

"Muldoon?" says Micaela. "Are you all right? You fainted."

"I'm fine," I reply, lifting myself up into a sitting position on the sofa that looks like cheese. "Better than fine. I'm elated!"

"You are?" Micaela's puzzled frown is adorable. "But just a minute ago you were complaining about all the rain we've been getting."

"I universe-hopped again from my home universe, where you were stillborn. You remember my previous visit, when I was tripping on Ink?"

For some reason, she seems less than thrilled to see me again.

"What's the matter?" I ask.

"What you don't seem to realize is that when you drop by this universe, in order to prevent the absurdity of encountering yourself here, my Muldoon is transported to *your* universe." Micaela sighs. "The last time that happened, he was scolded by some woman named Fannie Mae, threatened with bodily harm by a pugnacious ghostwriter, and intermittently found himself unable to think rationally. He said the only good thing about the place was his pet parrot."

This is bad news, indeed. The last time I was here, I simply assumed that the other Muldoon was spending the night away from home. It never occurred to me that the two of us had *switched universes*. How the hell am I supposed to tell Micaela that her Muldoon was just strangled to death by my lunatic uncle?

"I'm sure he'll be fine," I lie. "I've really cleaned up my act."

"Glad to hear it," says Micaela. "How did you get here? Ink again?"

I feel terrible about misleading my sister, but what's one more fib at this point? "I've been so desperate to see you again that I've been taking Ink nearly every day, but until today it's always landed me in the wrong damn universe. I count myself lucky to have escaped from some of them alive."

Micaela is so impressed by my bravery and my devotion to her that she wraps her arms around me in a giant bear hug. The warmth of her embrace and the intoxicating fragrance she exudes nearly cause me to swoon, and, overcome with emotion, I tell her that I love her more than I've ever loved anyone in my life.

The two of us celebrate our reunion by ordering out for Vernulian, and after feasting once again on luscious pampanus and succulent makmaks, along with a fine bottle of Grandiol—like Champagne, but tastier—we fall into each other's arms and share a kiss so delicious that I can hardly bear it.

"I suppose we should control ourselves," says Micaela. "I don't want to make you uncomfortable."

"Well, since I last saw you, my position on incest between consenting adult siblings has...evolved," I say. "As you said, if we're careful to use birth control, what's the big deal? Anyhow, when in Rome..."

As she takes my hand and leads me to her bedroom, I fuel my mounting desire by imagining I'd actually grown up with Micaela. Not in *her* universe, but in mine, where shagging your sister is considered the height of perversity, superseded only by fucking a goat, a child, or perhaps a cadaver.

We shed our clothes, fall into bed, and entwine our naked bodies, and as I caress Micaela and inhale her sweet and pungent scents, memories flood my mind that must belong to the Muldoon I've replaced. There we are as kids, building a sandcastle, sharing a bubble bath, playing house, catching fireflies on a warm summer evening. As teens, gossiping about schoolmates, prepping for exams, screaming at each other, and sharing our first tentative kiss. And as young adults, intimate phone calls late into the night, ferocious arguments, wild make-up sex, and mourning together the loss of our parents.

Micaela takes me in her mouth, and I shudder with exquisite pleasure as she repeatedly brings me to the brink and relents just in time. I return the favor, teasing her with hummingbird flicks of my tongue. When she can hold off no longer, Micaela draws me up and we luxuriate in a kiss as she guides me inside her.

The feeling is indescribable. We settle into a rhythm that matches that of our beating hearts, gasping as we melt into each other. We flow effortlessly from one position to the next, neither of us aware of taking the lead. The tempo gradually accelerates until we teeter on the edge of rapture. Micaela and I are so attuned to each other's needs, so telepathically linked, that it's as if two halves of a single person—separated for eons—have finally joined together in ecstatic delight.

Cuddling in bed afterward, I begin to feel sad and guilty.

"What's wrong?" asks Micaela. "There's something you're not telling me, isn't there?" The downside of her exquisite attunement to me now becomes apparent.

Realizing that it's pointless to try to keep a secret from her, I nod. "I lied to you about your Muldoon. He won't be returning."

"What do you mean?" Micaela sits up in bed. "I thought Ink only lasts for a day."

"I didn't take Ink this time. Jesus, haven't you read *Incognolio*, for crying out loud?"

"Of course. Several versions. But in none of them do I lose my Muldoon."

I'm about to ask Micaela for some whiskey when I remember that I don't drink in this universe. I'll have to forge ahead unaided. "You see, I took a class in universe-hopping. It involves this radical technique in which you envision your universe of choice at the exact moment that you die."

Micaela stares at me, unblinking.

"The instructor never mentioned that I'd be trading places with my counterpart. Otherwise, I never would have—"

"What are you saying? My Muldoon is *dead*?"

I nod.

Micaela gets up and walks out of the room. Through the open bedroom door I watch her fling herself down on the sofa in the other room, and I can hear her sobbing.

All I wanted was to be together with my beloved sister for the rest of my life. Now I'm a fucking monster who has murdered Micaela's true love. How can I even hope that she'll ever forgive me?

Micaela's crying suddenly stops. Then I hear a familiar chuckle, and look up to find Laszlo perched on a chair in the corner of the bedroom.

"Stinking scumbag!" I cry. "How the fuck did you find me?"

"You amaze me, Muldoon," he says. "Have you forgotten yet again that I'm writing this thing?"

"Okay, I give up. Kill me, for Christ's sake. Put me out of my misery."

"Too easy," says Laszlo. "I've already managed to murder—in order of appearance—Dr. Noggin, Yiddle, Lefty and Righty, Ko, Delphia, Hrabal, Mr. and Mrs. Yankerhousen, Myrtle Grouse, J.R. Cosmipolitano, President Peter Pecker, Greazly, Areola, Fannie May, Dick Fracken, Dr. Miranda, Dr. Schmendrik, the Kajoob, Arielle, Grunt, Quenchley, Malena, Babaganu (aka Raza LaRat), Ol' Man McNergal, Smirnoff, Jack, Paula, Piper, Paige, Baraka, Scout, Cassandra Didymos, Chester, Yazzle, Pizza Guy, Schlomo, Minor Character, the Dildorphians, Gemina, Dr. Heydar Ramazan, Phil, Misha Slodkin, Dean, Quodon, Angelica, Dr. Menos, Kurt, Grunion Horniak, President Donald Dork, Boudreaux, Floreska, Lunaria, the Shazan, Nameless One, Dr. Djinn, Deedle, Cecil Vernax, Dunkin, and President Rod Shaft. Now that Micaela's been snuffed out, you're my last character. You need to go out with a bang."

I glance through the open door, and sure enough, there is Micaela's lifeless body on the carpet. What's left of my heart implodes.

"Let's see." Laszlo strokes his chin as he thinks out loud. "I've always wanted to tar and feather someone, so we'll definitely start with that. Then I'll parade you down Mane Street, where people can hurl overripe fruit and rotten eggs at you as they taunt you mercilessly. Next, I'll hire a crane that can latch onto your testicles and lift you high into the air, while sharp shooters use you for target practice, firing rubber bullets that break bones, but aren't fatal. Back on the ground, you'll be anally violated by a stallion while—"

"Hold on!" Compelled either by fear or by the last traces of my life instinct—or perhaps I'm still unwilling to give up authorship of this manuscript—I refuse to bow out just yet. "I'm not your last character standing. How about Incognolio and Mazazel?"

"Well, I wouldn't exactly call them characters." Laszlo chuckles, a bit nervously. "After all, they're more like Gods or forces of Nature."

"Still, you invented them, didn't you?"

"That goes without saying." Laszlo recovers himself, and puts on a brave smile. "But I'll dispose of them later. First, I'll devise new and exciting ways to humiliate you to your dying breath."

"Ah, but consider, dear uncle, that you may yet have some need of me. No doubt you can take out Mazazel by yourself, but when it comes to Incognolio...well, you're simply too loathsome to get anywhere near her. Whereas she'll be only too happy to receive me, at which point I can destroy her from within."

"Hmm, that actually makes sense," says Laszlo. "But why would you want to help *me*?"

"As a lifelong lover of literature, let's just say that I want to make sure that you nail your ending."

"Fair enough," says Laszlo. "Let's roll. I'll meet you back here once we've vanquished those two antediluvian muckety-mucks."

CHAPTER THIRTY-SIX

UNDERWORLD

Pleased with myself for having pulled one over on Muldoon, I usher him out of the room, close the door, and take a seat on the bed as I wait for my nephew to return from dispatching Incognolio.

I have no intention of holding up my end of the deal, since I have no interest in destroying Mazazel. He is, after all, my benefactor, the hero of my story, and the source of my bottomless evil, not to mention the namesake of my great opus.

Still, I need to report back, so I summon the Dark Lord and he immediately materializes, appearing more repulsive and grotesque than ever.

"I have accomplished everything you requested, Master." I fill my lungs, reveling in the nauseating stench that emanates from the Archfiend. "And as soon as Muldoon returns from his mission, you shall reign supreme."

"Excellent, Laszlo." Mazazel rubs together his wart-ridden, pus-covered hands with glee. "Now that I have no more use for you, I'm free to dispatch your miserable ass into eternal torment."

"But...but...I still need to kill Muldoon!"

"That delectable task shall be reserved for me."

"But you promised that I shall live forever as your apprentice and confidante!" I hate the whining tone of my voice, hate that I feel crushed and betrayed—

Mazazel erupts in riotous laughter. "You ought to know better than anyone that my promises are worthless."

—and most of all, I hate that I didn't see this coming. I have been taken for a fool, and I'm livid. "What will be my fate?" I ask.

"Perhaps I'll start with that humiliating program of torture you devised for Muldoon," Mazazel replies. "Good stuff."

I grudgingly accept the compliment. I am nothing if not inventive, so maybe I can still concoct a way out of this predicament.

I have little time to reflect, however, since Mazazel gets right to work, and by the time I've been tarred, feathered, hoisted, shot at, and penetrated by horse-meat, I'm still struggling to come up with a plan.

After careful consideration, Mazazel decides to kill me via dismemberment. He starts with my hair, which he pulls out in bunches, then moves on to my finger- and toenails, using pliers to extract them, one by one. The pain is excruciating, but I simply laugh, partly to provoke Mazazel, but also because it feels good.

Annoyed, Mazazel wastes no time in breaking off each of my digits and snipping off my genitals, but not before pulverizing each of my balls with a nutcracker.

"Bring it on, you old fart," I say. "Don't you realize that I thrive on pain?"

This is the truth. For me, pain is pleasure. But I am also taunting Mazazel, figuring that with enough goading I might be able to enrage him to the point that he self-destructs.

"Stop leering at me, you moron!" shouts Mazazel, and he swiftly gouges out my eyes. When this elicits nothing from me but a ghastly grin, he proceeds to yank out each of my teeth.

"Id dat da bess you can do?" I say. "Wad a cweam puff!"

Infuriated, Mazazel finally silences me by tearing out my tongue. In a frenzy, he hacks off my limbs, splits me down the middle from my sternum to my pubic bone, rips out my intestines, liver, kidneys, spleen, pancreas, and lungs, and finishes me off by snatching out my beating heart and devouring it.

I am transported to the Underworld, where the atmosphere of evil that suffuses the place feels like home to me, and the relentless shrieks and wails of countless souls in agony are music to my ears. Ah, and the darkness, the sweet and total darkness! This complete and utter absence of light and love is something I find profoundly soothing.

My reconstituted body— etheric rather than physical—is even more acutely sensitive to pain and other sensations. I experience both the freezing cold of absolute zero and a scorching heat that burns hundreds of times hotter than any earthly fire. My body is afflicted with painful diseases, flaming maggots crawl in and out of every orifice, my hunger and thirst know no bounds, and dense clouds of stifling smoke choke me with every breath. Demons torture me—whipping me, piercing me, and submerging me in boiling oil. Imps mock and humiliate me, insult me, and hurl excrement and every manner of filth at me. Wild beasts and hideous monsters attack and mutilate me, leaving my body in shreds. All the while, I am never permitted to escape even momentarily into sleep.

Periodically, Mazazel checks in on me, and I make sure to let him know that not only is he failing to break my spirit, he's empowering me.

"Why are you going so easy on me?" I complain. "More pain!"

"Damn it! How can that be?" Mazazel erupts like a volcano, producing a deafening roar that resounds throughout the Underworld. "How can you tolerate such torment?"

"Don't you understand anything?" I laugh until tears fill my eyes. "I loathe and despise myself so thoroughly that the harsher the punishment, the better I feel!"

Mazazel is so beside himself with rage that I begin to think my plan might actually work, that he will annihilate himself in one enormous burst of super-charged fury.

But as Author Laszlo sits in his study at work on *Mazazel*, imagining this blast of boundless rage and trying to capture it in words, he suddenly experiences a massive heart attack, keels over, and dies.

CHAPTER THIRTY-SEVEN

THE ETERNAL NOW

Pleased with myself for having duped Laszlo, since I intend to *merge* with the Goddess Incognolio, not destroy her, I walk into the living room and over to Micaela. I stoop, lift her limp body, and transfer it to the sofa, then arrange her hair and close her eyelids. Sick with grief, I gently kiss her lips one last time while tears cascade down my cheeks. I would like to give her a decent burial, but I must turn my attention to figuring out how to locate Incognolio. So I leave Micaela on the couch, sit down at the desk, and boot up the computer.

The only lead I have is that Misha discovered Incognolio by taking the psychedelic drug, Anosh. I type that term into a search engine and find, to my dismay, that in this universe Anosh is not a mind-expanding drug, but rather the brand name of an ointment for treating acne.

For the hell of it, I type the term *Incognolio* into the search box. I scroll through several pages of results—mostly reviews of my novel and websites where it's sold—and I come across a listing for the Incognolio Book Club, which meets this very evening on the sixth floor of the Literary Arts Building. Hoping to cross paths with someone who might be able to point me in the right direction, I decide to attend.

It's raining outside, so I throw on a trench coat and grab an umbrella before walking downstairs and out the door. I have a beer and something called *fish and dreck* at a local pub, then head over to the Literary Arts Building, which is exactly where I suspected it might be.

In room 639, where the meeting has just begun, I quietly take a seat, joining a circle of about fifteen people. The leader of the proceedings, an odd-looking woman who introduces herself as Hardwood Florence, welcomes everyone and announces that tonight's focus will be on the novel's ending.

"Personally, I was disappointed," says a jaundiced man to my right. "I thought the author owed it to us to finally clear up all of those unresolved plotlines."

"But doesn't all the uncertainty mirror what we encounter in our daily lives?" asks a woman wearing mushroom earrings. "We just muddle onward, and hardly anything ever gets resolved one way or the other."

"You both are missing the point," says a fulsome woman to my left. "The novel focuses the reader on the Eternal Now, which is free of the past, the future, and of linear time itself. It's like those intricate Tibetan sand paintings that take several days to construct. The monks destroy them shortly after completion, as a metaphor for the impermanence of existence."

"Precisely," chimes in a man wearing a wool hat in the shape of a beaver. "Quantum physics demonstrates that time and causality are illusions. Everything that *can* happen *does* happen. That's why there is no single authoritative ending to the novel. Each copy that's published has a different ending."

"Or, as Oscar Wilde put it," says Hardwood Florence, "books are never finished, they are merely abandoned."

Florence turns to me for my opinion, and I admit that I haven't finished reading the novel yet, and am wondering if anyone can tell me how Muldoon manages to find the Goddess Incognolio.

"Wait a minute—" says the fulsome woman, flipping to the photo on the last page of her copy. "*You're* the author! You're Muldoon!"

Well, this is embarrassing, and it leaves me wishing I'd worn some sort of disguise. The atmosphere in the room is charged with excitement, as each of the members in turn has me sign their copy of the novel and then takes a selfie with me. Finally, when everyone has returned to their seats, one member asks why I don't know what happens in my own book.

"Ah," I say. "I can see how that could seem confusing. The truth is that I'm from an alternate universe in which I haven't finished writing the manuscript."

"No offense," says mushroom woman, "but I don't see why it even matters whether or not you find Incognolio. The book's already in print, after all."

"I'm aware of that," I say. "But I still have a life of my own, you know, apart from the novel."

"Oh, my," says Hardwood Florence. "You really haven't learned a thing, have you? And here I thought Pizza Guy had succeeded in convincing you that Author Muldoon and Protagonist Muldoon are equally fictitious."

"Look," I say, "I didn't come here to get embroiled in ontological debates. I simply want to know if anyone can tell me how to locate the Goddess Incognolio."

"That's easy," says beaver hat. "Just leave in a huff."

And that's exactly what I do.

Only after I'm outside getting drenched do I realize that I left my umbrella behind. I'd prefer not to go back into that room, but the rain is coming down so hard that I have little choice. I take the elevator to the sixth floor, but when the doors open, not only isn't the carpet the same color as before, there's no carpet at all. In fact, I'm staring out into empty space.

Without even a thought, I leap into the void and find myself falling in slow motion, just like Alice down the rabbit hole. As I fall, I can't help feeling that this is what I've been doing all along, from the very first sentence, leaping into the void, without a clue as to where I'm headed, taking it on faith that things will somehow work themselves out in the end.

Whether I've been falling for an hour or a century I cannot say, but at some point, I hear the far-off voice of Incognolio calling out to me. It's the sweetest, most soulful voice I've ever heard in my life. And as her voice grows louder, I no longer feel like I'm falling, but rather that I am being drawn inside Incognolio, letting go of my identity as Muldoon and gradually merging with the Goddess. It is just as I described it in my novel.

At first, it's sheer ecstasy surrendering my boundaries and expanding into the limitless freedom of Incognolio. I allow all my pain and guilt, my sadness and despair, to simply melt away. This leaves me completely unburdened as I open myself to the ocean of love that envelops me, immerses me in the unconditional affection and acceptance for which I've longed my entire life.

And yet, as wonderful as it feels, some part of me finds such love intolerable. Like my father, Misha—who I invented, after all—I find myself resisting Incognolio, pushing her away, telling her that I don't deserve such joy and rapture. At bottom I am bad, having killed Micaela's Muldoon and indirectly caused Micaela's death, having spent my life drinking and carousing, lying to everyone including myself, pushing away women who just wanted to love me. In short, that I'm a miserable wretch, unworthy of what Incognolio offers.

The Goddess will not force me to merge with her, nor can she magically eradicate my self-loathing. Instead she releases me, and as I slowly emerge from her succoring embrace, I realize that only two alternatives remain: I must return to my miserable life or, even worse, be thrown into Mazazel's monstrous Underworld.

And as Author Muldoon sits in his study, imagining this agonizing bind and trying to capture the dilemma in words, he suddenly suffers a grand mal seizure, keels over, and dies.

CHAPTER THIRTY-EIGHT

NAMELESS ONE

After countless eons of nothingness, I was so bored out of my mind I couldn't bear even just a trillion more years of Nonbeing. So I created two deities, Incognolio and Mazazel. At first it was marvelous, so astounded was I by their inventiveness, so astonished by their spontaneity, so entertained by their games and tomfoolery, their witty banter, practical jokes, and tall tales.

Everything was idyllic until, one day, Mazazel went a little overboard with his teasing and hurt Incognolio's feelings. She wept her first tears, a torrent of them, and Mazazel, horrified at what he had done, hid himself away, struggling with the primordial stirrings of shame, guilt, and self-recrimination.

When Mazazel finally returned, no longer was he childlike or happy-go-lucky. Instead, he began to brood and think dark thoughts, and despite all Incognolio's attempts to rekindle their closeness and show that she still loved him, Mazazel would have none of it. In fact, he began openly to taunt her, never missing an opportunity to embarrass and humiliate Incognolio, to wound and abuse her.

I watched as Mazazel became increasingly sadistic and learned to ward off intolerable feelings of self-hatred by projecting his badness onto the Other—Incognolio—and in this manner, he grew outrageously confident and full of himself. Mazazel became convinced it was *he* who was righteous and *she* who deserved harsher and harsher punishments, which he was only too happy to mete out, although they served, in fact, to deepen his unconscious self-loathing, creating a vicious cycle.

Meanwhile, as she managed to endure ever-greater dimensions of cruelty and torture, rather than stand up to Mazazel, Incognolio grew increasingly submissive, martyring herself, making excuses for her tormenter, and convincing herself that if only she loved him enough, she could rescue Mazazel, heal him, and ultimately transform him back into the sweet, compassionate Being he once was.

I considered intervening at this point, to prevent my offspring from suffering. But I was curious to see what would happen if I left them to their own devices, and I enjoyed assuming the role of detached spectator, observing from a distance. Not to mention that I had grown weary of their fun and games and found these dramatic new developments far more compelling.

Over the ages, Incognolio and Mazazel played out every scenario imaginable, repeated ad nauseam, until finally, out of desperation, they created the physical universe, with its trillions of stars, including the sun, and its quadrillions of planets, including the earth, and as if that weren't enough, they fashioned an infinite number of alternate universes.

Fascinated, I witnessed that on Earth, as on every other planet where intelligent life evolved, Incognolio and Mazazel were able to breathe new life into their dramas, now one step removed, as vast numbers of sentient beings played out the comedies and tragedies of their existence, struggling to negotiate the dual influences of Mazazel and Incognolio.

Even better, as the various cultures developed storytelling—first in oral form, then in written—an endless variety of fictional narratives were produced, captivating me with their creativity and suspense, delighting me with their wit, challenging me with their insight and profundity.

But there can be too much of a good thing. At this point I feel glutted and overstimulated, having been exposed to every conceivable plot, story line, adventure, anecdote, fable, fantasy, myth, allegory, cliff-hanger, potboiler, folktale, parable, parody, farce, romance, and fairytale that can or ever will be devised. So it's time to close up shop, draw the curtains, lay down the pen, and pull the plug, bringing this round of Being to an end.

I heave a colossal sigh and call Incognolio and Mazazel to my side, informing them that the time has come at last for them to disappear.

Mazazel and Incognolio wail and moan. They beg me—O, Nameless One—to reconsider; put forth every sort of argument, disputation, and polemic; promise that they will try harder, be more creative, come up with better stories; and even threaten to depose me. But it's too late, my patience has run out. I am fed up with the hustle and whirl of Being and long only for silence, sweet silence, and for the deep dreamless sleep of oblivion.

CHAPTER THIRTY-NINE

DR. DICK

That's all well and good, you think to yourself. But where does that leave *me,* the Not-So-Gentle Reader of this tale, who sees that the story is drawing to a close, and—whether saddened at the prospect or relieved by it—wants to know what message to take away from the novel.

"That's entirely up to you," I say. "Each reading of the text is unique."

"Don't give me that crap, Sussman," you reply. "You're obviously trying to say *something,* so why not just come right out and say it?"

"My take on the novel is irrelevant," I say. "Haven't you read *The Death of the Author* by Roland Barthes? He says the essential meaning of a text depends on the impressions of the *reader.* The author exists solely to produce the work, not explain it."

"How convenient! Perhaps I should collect your royalties as well."

"Perhaps." I smile.

"So let me get this straight. Are you saying you had no authorial intentions whatsoever?"

"Hey, I just started with the title, *Incognolio*, and kept on writing. If I had any intentions, my friend, they were purely unconscious."

"I don't believe that for a second. Even some of your characters offer interpretations of the proceedings."

"I take no responsibility for what my characters do or say. You know damn well that they take on lives of their own."

"Oh, yeah? Then maybe I'll just grab your butt-ugly head and shove it down this toilet, you lying sack of—"

I sigh and start over. I'm determined to get this right, but the odds are stacked against me.

Given its unconventional structure, this story presents a unique challenge when it comes to devising an appropriate ending. Having intentionally left plotlines unresolved, I can't turn around and offer a nice, tidy, conventional ending in which so many errant roadways neatly converge on a final and gratifying endpoint. A novel that has systematically defied the reader's expectations cannot suddenly seek to satisfy them.

In addition, the conclusion of a novel should feel inevitable. But how can I establish a sense of inevitability when the tale has meandered in such a random fashion?

Moreover, I am no closer to comprehending the meaning of Incognolio than I was on page one. At best, I can assert that it can never be understood. Like *incognito*—I might point out—it derives from *incognitus*, the Latin word for *unknown*.

And finally, I have strong internal resistances to endings of any kind.

At a loss, I go to see my psychiatrist, Dr. Dick, the only person to have read my manuscript to this point.

"Okay, you're so goddamn smart." I fling a check for last month's sessions at him and we both take a seat. "Why can't I write a decent ending?"

"I detect a note of hostility," says Dr. Dick.

"No shit," I reply. "I've been seeing you twice a week for nearly a decade, and where has it got me? If I had any balls, I'd report you to your licensing board."

"You are a deeply disturbed individual." Dr. Dick carefully folds the check and pockets it. "Without my assistance, you would have killed yourself long ago."

"Thank you for making my point! I never *asked* you for help in keeping me alive. Au contraire, I made it clear from the start that my goal is to commit suicide."

"But as you are well aware, Mr. Sussman, your father is paying for this treatment. And *he* wants me to keep you alive."

As much as I'd like it to be otherwise, the check I handed Dr. Dick was written by my father, who at the age of eighty-three continues to support me financially, in exchange for which I agree to remain in therapy.

"I'm not a child," I say. "You work for *me*, not my fucking father."

"As you know, Michael, my Hippocratic Oath prevents me from doing harm, so I'd be acting unethically were I to assist you in ending your life."

It is at this moment that it dawns on me: My inability to end the novel is entangled with my inability to kill myself. For years now, the one thing that's kept me alive is a grim determination to finish this book. As soon as it's complete, I'll have no more excuses.

"So that's why you've slammed every single ending I've written," I say. "You don't *want* me to finish the damn book."

"Nonsense." Dr. Dick clears his throat, then straightens his tie. "I've told you time and again that your inability to conclude the novel derives from your unresolved Oedipal complex. Unconsciously, you fear that surpassing your father or competing with him in any way will bring punishment or abandonment. Therefore, you sabotage your own success and remain subservient to him."

"Spare me your Freudian dogma, dickhead." I get up to leave.

"We still have thirty minutes, Michael. Your rebellious attitude resembles that of an adolescent, who defies authority figures to conceal underlying feelings of impotent rage."

"You want to see rage?" I dash over to Dr. Dick and grab him by the neck. "I'll show you rage."

I proceed to strangle my doctor, squeezing his throat as he flails his arms and gasps for breath, reveling in the sense of power and vitality that infuses my being. I've never felt so alive in all my life, and decide that as soon as I've murdered Dr. Dick, I'll head straight over to my father's house and kill him, too.

CHAPTER FORTY

GEMMA

And now I must grudgingly admit that there *is* no Dr. Dick, nor have I ever subjected myself to the trickery and psychic violation known as psychotherapy. Moreover, I've really got no idea whether or not my father is still alive, on account of his having abandoned me and my twin sister, Gemma, when we were four. Perhaps it was that unspeakable loss that was the genesis of my compulsive lying, which has graduated to a vocation. Growing up, I found myself telling other kids that my papa was an explorer who embarked on an expedition—in one version to the North Pole, in another to the center of the earth, and in yet another to the moon.

And since at long last I'm being honest, it's essential to reveal that the whole time I've been writing this novel, I kept it from my sister, with whom I've lived my entire adult life, because I'm certain that she'll be horrified by the incest scenes and will insist that I remove them.

Such a request would place me in a horrendous bind.

If I refuse, Gemma might never forgive me. Might even leave me. I'd lose my best friend, my lover, my goddamn soul mate. All over a stupid book.

But if I comply, expunging every reference to incest—my metaphor for reunion with the split-off self—I'd be tearing out the very soul of my novel, in which I've invested the proverbial blood, sweat, and tears, not to mention several other bodily fluids.

In a cowardly attempt to delay a confrontation with Gemma, I extend my manuscript, adding chapters, concocting further scenarios, figuring out new ways to avoid reaching the end.

But now that I think about it, I realize that I'm using an imagined conflict with my sister to avoid facing my own ambivalence about going public with the truth. After all, what if I've misjudged Gemma? What if she doesn't object to the scenes in question? Doesn't even object to my identifying her in this chapter? If I knew she approved, would I then have no qualms about completing the manuscript and sending it off to my agent?

Of course not. Because...

One, I'm deeply ashamed.

Two, I know I'll be treated like a pariah.

And three, I don't really have an agent, do I? After all, what agent in her right mind would take on a client who is a pathological liar? A man who either is a perverted sister-fucker or, perhaps worse, labors creatively to give the impression that he's a perverted sister-fucker.

Indeed, what agent would willingly represent a novel that lacks a cohesive plot, a recognizable setting, characters with any depth, or a viable ending?

Suddenly I'm furious.

At the publishing industry, which has repeatedly snubbed me and refuses to take a risk on material that dares to be extraordinary.

At Gemma, who treats me like an invalid and refuses to be open with others about the nature of our relationship.

And most of all at myself, for ever starting this project and letting Incognolio, that insidious word, burrow into and colonize my brain, spreading through my gray matter like a cancer, expanding in scope until I can think of nothing else but the proliferating meanings of that diabolical word, which forever evades definition and identification and taunts me like a temptress who works me into a frenzy and then leaves me high and dry.

Well, no more!

There's one surefire way to cast out Incognolio for good and end this torment: Blow my fucking brains out.

CHAPTER FORTY-ONE

FADE TO WHITE

After months of mourning, Gemma finds herself perusing *Incognolio*, and even though she despises Michael's novel because it was the instrument of his demise, she feels that the story captures his spirit and therefore decides to publish it.

She sends queries to a handful of agents, selecting those who are open to transgressive tales that don't fit neatly into established genres. But all she gets back are form-letter rejections, so she sends out another batch, and another—all with the same result, leaving her angry and dejected, unable to comprehend why no one will so much as read the damn thing.

Then one day she receives an email from an entity named Quodon, bearing a subject heading that reads: **Urgent Message!** The dispatch is quite lengthy, so she decides to print it out, even though she has reason to suspect that she's low on printer ink. It reads:

Dearest Gemma,

Do not despair. In what Earthlings perceive as present time, most of you are not ready for the novel titled Incognolio. Within twenty Earth years, however, it will be widely acclaimed as a comic tour de force.

How do I know this?

Because here in Incognolio—the dimension in which I reside—we are no longer slaves to linear time and instead have equal access to what you call the past and future. It was I, you see, who acted as your brother's muse and guided the unfolding of his novel.

I hope you will be comforted by the news that although Michael is deceased in your dimension, here he is very much alive, and is anxious for you to join us. If you wish to be reunited with your brother, we would be delighted to transport you to Incognolio, where existence is more wondrous than your wildest imaginings.

Why, just yesterday—or was it tomorrow?—Michael was in the middle of frabulating his janx, when those rascals Bellyrumple and Schmerka dropped by and whisked him off to Level Seven, conjecturing it was high time that he experienced his first Transmogulation. After a light meal of luscious pampanus and makmaks, Michael was given a whiffling and fitted for an Alpha-Omega suit. No sooner had your brother plunged into the Flurge than wave after wave of euphoria cascaded through his neuroganglia, releasing every last trace of negativity and self-loathing accumulated during his numerous lifetimes on Earth, Knarval, and Zirconium, propelling him through the Vorpal Haze and the Ecstatisphere, headlong into the White Light of Incog

CHAPTER FORTY-TWO

CRAGAHOOCHIE, STRAIGHT UP

The fade out was a stroke of genius, allowing me to wrap up the novel without having to write an actual ending. In my mind, I liken it to the final line of Finnegans Wake, cut off mid-sentence to form an ouroboric loop with the opening word.

After making some minor revisions—the manuscript seemed nearly perfect—I did my research, cherry-picked ten so-called *dream agents*, and queried them, attaching the opening chapters. It was several weeks before I had received responses from all ten—brief form letters which I pinned to my dart board—but I wasn't fazed in the least, and with each rejection I simply dispatched two new queries. When this second round of queries bombed, I grew impatient and began contacting agents indiscriminately.

Eight months of mounting rage ensued. By then I'd pitched *Incognolio* to upwards of two hundred literary agents, and not one of those cowardly cunts dared represent it. Several of them praised the writing, using such terms as *tremendous, blue-ribbon, exciting, innovative,* and *extremely creative.* But they considered the novel far too quirky and edgy for mainstream publishers.

Looking back on it, even allowing for the elation one experiences on completing a creative project, the mystery is how I ever imagined that I might succeed in the first place.

Me, whose life had amounted to little more than an endless parade of defeats, humiliations, and failures. Somehow I'd convinced myself that by writing without censoring or forethought, by flinging open the gates to my subconscious, I could not only create a brilliant novel, but free myself of my demons in the process.

Yeah, right.

So here I sit in my study, faced with a worthless manuscript and an aborted metamorphosis that has left me even more alienated and disturbed than before I started the project. Disgusted with myself, I forsake my couch and throw on a jacket, aiming to head over to Banister's and get plastered.

The phone rings just as I reach the front door, but by the time I pick up the receiver, I hear Gemma talking about me to a woman whose voice I can't quite place.

I hang up and, after stewing over it for a while, storm into my sister's bedroom to confront her.

"Who the hell was that?"

"Oh, just a telemarketer." Gemma rises from bed and, without so much as glancing at me, enters the walk-in closet.

"I've heard her voice before, Gemma. You mentioned my goddamn name."

"I see," says Gemma from inside the closet. "So, you've been eavesdropping."

"No!" I try to calm myself. "Jesus, Gem. What the hell are you hiding?"

Gemma sighs, and even though I'm pissed, I can't help but savor the sweet sound. She emerges from the closet clutching a floral caftan and fleece leggings, her face a study in sheepish contrition, which I don't buy for a second.

"Sit down," she says.

I squint at her and remain standing.

"Have it your way." She slips out of her kimono, sits on the bed fully naked, and pulls on the leggings. "I've been in touch with Lamia."

Our cousin Lamia was the only child of Fallopia, my maternal aunt. I'd heard from Gemma that Lamia had recently established herself as a freelance editor, having been laid off from MacGuffin Press during the recession.

"In touch?" I ask.

"About *Incognolio*."

"*What*? How the hell do you even know—"

"I used to read the manuscript while you napped."
I glare at Gemma as she finishes dressing. As twins and
housemates, Gemma and I have almost no secrets, and
the manuscript was the one place I could express myself freely, without concern for my sister's feelings or
judgments. "I'm sorry, Mick, but I've watched you de-
teriorate lately, and I thought it might have to do with
your writing."

"You had no right. That's a violation of privacy."

"If you want privacy, you're free to move out."

I fume silently as Gemma fetches a pair of espa-
drille heels, returns to the bed, and slips them on, making damn sure I get a good long look at her soft soles
and long perfect toes. My sister is nothing if not consistent in how she seduces, manipulates, and ultimately
rejects me.

"What's Lamia got to do with it?" I finally ask.

"I've hired her to evaluate your manuscript."

"You what? It's *my* novel, damn it. You're not my
goddamn mother!"

"Maybe Lamia can figure out why you can't find an
agent."

"I *know* why, Gem. They think the story's too bizarre. Too unconventional."

"Yes, but what if Lamia can help you make it so compelling, so sublime, that none of that matters?"

As my fury subsides, the sense underlying Gemma's idea begins to sink in. Perhaps what I needed all along was a fresh pair of eyes, someone to point out the novel's weaknesses and suggest revisions.

"How far along is she?" I ask.

"She's done. She called to see if you can get together with her today. I said you'll meet her in half an hour at Banister's."

"Then why did you lie when I asked you who called?"

"Just having some fun. You should try it some time."

I curse Gemma up and down, but I'm secretly excited to meet with my cousin, who has edited fiction for nearly two decades.

In no time, I find myself sitting across from her in a booth at Bannister's Tavern. She looks eerily like photographs of my late aunt when she was younger, with the same mischievous blue eyes and crooked grin.

Banister limps over and awaits our orders.

"A mimosa for me," says Lamia. "And a Jack Daniels on the rocks, I presume, for my cousin."

"Tennessee whiskey for Mr. Sussman?" Banister cackles. "Cragahoochie, straight up, no doubt."

I nod to Banister and explain to Lamia that *Incognolio* is only minimally autobiographical. "Neither Muldoon nor the character named Michael Sussman are anything like me."

"No kidding," says Lamia. Her expression makes it all too obvious that she thinks I'm full of it.

Banister delivers our drinks and we clink glasses.

"So, give it to me straight," I say. "Is it rubbish?"

"I so love this book, Michael. It's engaging and haunting, interesting and clever, subtly layered. I feel honored to work with you on it."

"Isn't that laying it on a bit thick?" I say.

"I'm being entirely honest. I know that you're feeling discouraged because you haven't had any luck querying it, but this manuscript is already strong, and I have some ideas for improving it."

"Go on."

She drones on for several minutes, presenting several suggestions that would be tedious to implement, and their dubious value makes it highly unlikely that I will attempt any of them. It's no wonder MacGuffin fired her.

Her last point, however, does bear consideration. "Finally, Michael, I'm guessing that you've been pitching *Incognolio* as a comic novel."

"You don't think it's funny?"

"It's hilarious," says Lamia. "But despite its playfulness, your story's a tragedy."

I sip my drink and gesture for her to continue.

"I believe the Author's true design starts to become clear in Paige's narrative about her mystical and sexual union with her twin sister. The Author seeks union with himself.

"To achieve this integration, to cross that threshold into the dark and uncharted recesses of his subconscious, the Author would need to be willing to embrace his monsters, including the source of his self-loathing. It would require him to be his whole, true self without shame or fear."

"Tall order," I say. Lamia's smile looks forced.

"The tragedy is that he can't face his monsters, can't find a strategy for confronting the things he's most afraid of. Unable to successfully complete the novel, he self-destructs."

I sit quietly for several minutes, mulling over Lamia's take on the book and wondering why I feel so annoyed with her.

"Your reading of the story makes sense," I admit. "But you've got it all wrong."

"How so?"

"I stripped myself *naked* in those pages! Exposed my most deviant thoughts, my most depraved impulses. And I resisted *every* damn urge to gloss over the vile shit that gurgled up from the depths of my psyche. So don't sit there on your high fucking horse and tell me that I choked."

"This is good." Another phony smile. "We need to be open and honest if we're going to work together."

"Did Gemma hire you as an editor or as my damn therapist?" I grumble, and grow sullen. Lamia signals Banister for another round.

"It took courage and grit to write your manuscript," she says. "That's undeniable. But what I'm suggesting, Michael, is that at the last moment you pull back, just as Muldoon and Misha both shrink from merging with the Goddess Incognolio."

I don't know what to say. I'd just allowed the story to flow out of me and had never really tried to *analyze* it before.

"For instance, you portray Muldoon as self-loathing and highly self-destructive, a man awash in shame, guilt, and remorse. Yet we never really learn the source of all this self-hatred."

"Well he *does* admit to killing Micaela."

"Ah, the Ferris wheel." Lamia searches my eyes. "Now, I understand that you consider *Incognolio* to be purely fictional, Michael. But that incident was from your actual childhood, although in real life you managed to save your sister just before she fell."

"I'm aware of that. It's called poetic license, Lamia. Killing her off was more dramatic."

"Exactly. And Micaela's death at the hands of Muldoon provides a rationale for his lifelong emotional turmoil. But he's just a boy at the time, and he certainly didn't intend to kill her. Perhaps you could elevate the tension by having Muldoon repeatedly try to knock off his sister as they grow older. *You* know"—Lamia winks—"like you and Gemma?"

I scrutinize her. Just how much did Lamia know? She and Gemma were somewhat close, but I'd always assumed that Gemma kept certain things between the two of us.

"Sure, there might have been an incident or two." I knead the back of my neck. "But I wouldn't call it *repeatedly*."

"No? Okay, let's enumerate." Lamia presents her fist and sticks up her thumb. "About a year after the Ferris wheel incident, you nearly pushed Gemma down a wishing well."

"There was *plenty* of water at the bottom of that well." I try not to sound too defensive. "Hell, I measured it myself with a brick tied to a rope. There was a chance she'd drown, I suppose, but the fall was unlikely to kill her."

"Right." Lamia nods, straight-faced, and continues, extending her index finger. "And how about when you injected nightshade into Gemma's toothpaste? Was that just to help her overcome insomnia?"

"Very funny."

"Numbers three and four: a black mamba that mysteriously appeared under her bed sheets one evening, and a Cassoulet that you prepared using monkey brains and puffer fish. Then there was Giuliani, the rabid Chihuahua you adopted…"

I tune out, satisfied that I have learned the real reason Gemma chose Lamia to edit my manuscript. Not to help me, but so that she could confront me with past transgressions. Not to protect my fragile psyche from further deterioration, but to push me over the edge into the abyss!

CHAPTER FORTY-THREE

THE IDIOT'S GUIDE TO SUICIDE

We're on our third round of drinks, and despite my mounting mistrust of Lamia, I find myself lowering my guard as her questions become more personal.

"As an editor, I try to get inside my author's head," she remarks. "One question that I always like to ask is: What did you learn from writing your novel?"

"Let me think…" I reply. "Oh, right: That the sort of novel I like to write is impossible to sell?"

Lamia cracks a smile.

"I also learned that the creative process must be its own reward, since it doesn't bring external validation, and it sure as hell doesn't make you a better or happier person."

"Okay. What else?"

"Well…I suppose that whatever it is I'm searching for, either it doesn't exist or it's unobtainable. My pursuit of transcendence is pointless and can end only in frustration and despair."

She is silent for a moment, which gives me time to realize that our conversation has left me feeling morose and dejected, without giving me any good notions of how to revise the novel. Ready to be done with it, I signal Banister for the check.

But then Lamia says, "What struck me about your ending, Michael, is that despite the Author's realization that he has ultimately come up empty, he blames this failure entirely on external factors."

"How so?" I ask, taken aback.

"It's all Gemma's fault for treating the Author like an invalid and either rebuffing his advances or publicly denying what may or may not be an incestuous relationship. The fault lies with cowardly literary agents— no, *the entire publishing industry*—for snubbing the Author and refusing to take a risk on his cutting-edge, wildly-popular-in-an-alternate-universe novel. Finally, the Author blames his therapist, Dr. Dick, for his own inability to come up with a satisfying ending. But a satisfying ending can only happen if there is transformation, and the power to transform lies with the Author, not with his therapist."

Banister limps over with the check and I pay, waving away Lamia's outstretched bills. I've pretty much decided to fire my cousin and tell her to go to hell—she clearly doesn't know what she's talking about—but I can't resist one last attempt at defending myself.

"You'll note," I say, "that the Author doesn't just murder Dr. Dick. He proceeds to blow his own brains out."

"Yes, but then you tack on a light-hearted postscript that undoes his suicide. The Author, we learn, is alive and kicking, up to all sorts of hijinks in another dimension. Whoopee."

"I never cared for you, Lamia. But at this moment I detest you."

Lamia flashes her crooked grin, and I could punch her stinking face in.

"Fine, so the ending sucks," I say. "Instead of just tearing me down, how about telling me how to fix it?"

"Simple." Lamia locks eyes with me. "First, have the Author realize that what stands between him and what he wants is *himself*. He sees that he's unwilling or incapable of doing what it takes to achieve transformation. Because of this, the storytelling act is doomed to failure, and this simple fact drives him to insanity and death. And for crying out loud, come up with a more creative way to kill yourself—I mean...to kill the Author."

"There's a reason I chose a gun, smartass." I hesitate to reveal my rationale, since it sounds so *irrational*. Nevertheless, I proceed. "You'll probably think I'm nuts, but sometimes things I write in my novels come true. I used a gun to kill myself in the story because in real life, thanks to a history of mental illness, I can't acquire one."

"I see." Lamia mulls this over for a minute or two and then abruptly stands up. "I've got an idea. Let's go."

Lamia leads the way to a bus stop where we board the #33 bus. As we pass the cemetery, she laughs. "Where'd you come up with that image of the revolving graveyard?" she asks. "Seemed like something straight out of a Terry Gilliam film."

"I dreamed it. When I'm immersed in a story, my dreams and waking life can intertwine."

We approach the Seppuku Bridge, named for the famous Japanese architect who designed it, and Lamia pulls the overhead cord to signal the bus driver.

"Why are we getting out here?" I ask.

"This is where your novel's final scene takes place."

"Hey, are you editing the damn thing or writing it?"

"Reply hazy," she deadpans. "Try again later."

We emerge from the bus, cross the street, head out onto the bridge, and begin walking directly into a stiff wind. I take several paces along the raised sidewalk and then stop.

"What's wrong?" Lamia inquires.

"Dread of heights. I avoid bridges at all costs."

"So I've heard." Lamia chuckles, and in the semi-darkness I can't determine whether or not the malicious gleam in her eyes is a product of my imagination. "That's why it's the perfect mode of suicide for the Author. In real life, you'd never jump off a bridge."

This makes sense. I resume walking.

"So what's with this superstition of yours? Do you really believe that your writing can influence future events?"

"It's more like my subconscious attunes itself to a realm beyond linear time."

"Huh." Lamia is clearly unimpressed. "And what evidence do you have for this…notion?"

"In my YA novel, *Crashing Eden*, the protagonist's twelve-year-old brother, Elijah, is taunted and bullied so ruthlessly that he offs himself. I never managed to publish it, but a couple of months after I gave up trying, I came across an article about a boy in a nearby town who was persecuted to the point of suicide."

"But that happens all the time. It hardly—"

"His name was Elijah. He was twelve, Lamia, and like my character, he hung himself with a belt."

At this point we're about a quarter of the way across the bridge. I keep my eyes trained on the sidewalk ahead of me.

"Then, while writing the first draft of *Incognolio*, I needed Laszlo Skuntch—Misha's evil twin brother—to realize that he'd entered an alternate universe. As you know, I had him discover a portrait of Donald Dork hanging on the wall of a post office. This was about three years before Trump announced his candidacy for President of the United States, so the idea of that fuck-face becoming president seemed absurd and outlandish at the time."

"Now, not so much," says Lamia. "But couldn't both instances simply be coincidence?"

"Certainly," I replied. "But you have to understand that this has been going on since I first took creative writing in the sixth grade. Three months before Chernobyl, I handed in a short story about the meltdown of a nuclear power plant in a remote village in the Soviet Union."

"Jesus."

"Then in eighth grade I wrote a piece in which an author is assassinated for publishing a novel that was labeled blasphemous by Muslim leaders. Two months later, the Ayatollah Khomeini, Supreme Leader of Iran, issued a fatwa against Salman Rushdie for publishing *The Satanic Verses*."

"Damn," says Lamia. "I can see why you take this stuff seriously."

Now that we're halfway across the bridge, she halts and steers me around to face the bay. I grab the waist-high railing and hold on for dear life, my extremities starting to tremble. Why on earth did I let Lamia convince me to do this?

"Try opening your eyes," she says gently.

"I'd rather not."

"Come on, Michael. It'll help you write the scene."

Reluctantly, I open my eyes and gaze out at the bay, focusing on the horizon in an attempt to quell the rising panic.

"Okay, I want you to gradually lower your line of sight," says Lamia.

Grumbling all the while, I comply with Lamia's instructions, noticing the various yachts, schooners, trawlers, and barges making their way across the choppy seas. There's a considerable amount of fog, lending to the scene an eerie quality, which exacerbates my anxiety. As I continue to sweep my gaze downward, I grip the railing more tightly and my palms start to sweat. And when I look straight down, I instinctively shut my eyes.

"What are you feeling, Michael?"

"Like I want to go home."

"Okay, but try digging a bit deeper. I realize that you dislike introspection. But for the sake of your novel, you need to explore your fear of heights. Or is it *falling* that you truly fear?"

Uncertain how to reply, I reopen my eyes, and look down from a height of over two hundred feet. The strong and erratic wind currents have whipped the water—usually a dull green—into a turbulent canvas of scudding gray. A windsurfer in a wetsuit emerges from under the bridge.

"I suppose it's the falling. As a kid, my friends could never convince me to ride a rollercoaster or drop box. Hell, I wouldn't even go near a swing.

"What scared you?"

"Everything about it. The lack of control and freedom from all restraint. The shortness of breath, racing heart, and jangling nerves."

"In short," says Lamia, "everything that would let you know that you're truly alive."

"Yeah, yeah. But there's more to it than that. I also had nightmares of tumbling down a steep staircase. I was convinced that I'd die when I hit bottom."

"Okay, so you're afraid of falling to your death. But is that the only reason you're gripping that railing like we were in a hurricane?"

My knuckles are white as chalk. And no matter how hard I try, I can't loosen my grip.

"It's odd," I say, "but I think I'm also fighting off the impulse to jump."

"Now we're getting somewhere. So, a part of you wants to hop the railing and leap to your death."

"A *big* part." I sigh, relieved to have finally given voice to my irrational truth. "Hell, if it wasn't for Gemma, I'd greet death with a smile. But I know it would devastate her."

We stand silently. After some time, I feel Lamia's hand on my shoulder.

"There's something I need to tell you," she says. "You're not going to like it, Michael. But as the Man said, the truth shall set you free."

I'm pretty certain I know what Lamia's going to say, given the way my sister's been acting of late. Gemma's increasingly fed up with having to support me—financially *and* emotionally, since I refuse to submit to a shrink—and weary from decades of fending off amorous advances.

"I'm all ears," I say.

There's another long pause, and then Lamia eases me around so that we're face to face, her hands cupping my shoulders.

"Gemma isn't real," she whispers. "She's like an imaginary friend you created as a child and never outgrew because you couldn't accept that your twin sister was stillborn."

"Good one." I chuckle mirthlessly, sweeping Lamia's hands off my shoulders, and step away from her. "Look, if Gemma wants me to move out, I'll do it. She doesn't need to enlist you in this charade."

"I can only imagine how painful this is to hear, Michael. But I'm being serious. Gemma exists solely in your mind."

"Yeah?" Okay, joke's over. Now I'm pissed. "Tell me, who arranged for us to meet today?"

"I asked Banister to call me the next time you showed up as his bar. I work out of my apartment, which is two blocks from the Tavern."

"Then how in hell did you manage to read my manuscript?"

"The last time you were hospitalized for depression, Michael, your doctor prescribed electroconvulsive therapy. You were deemed incompetent to give or withhold consent, and as your closest living relative, I was appointed guardian."

"And what the fuck does that have to do with the price of beans in Bangor?"

"You may not recall it, since ECT often wipes out all memory of the shock treatments, but one of the conditions for discharge from the hospital was that you give me the password to your iCloud account. I'm supposed to monitor your writing for any signs of impending breakdown."

I wait for a tell, some sign that Lamia's bluffing, but she appears to be sincere. Her answers to my questions all sound plausible, but if what she's saying is true—

that my twin sister died at birth and Gemma is imaginary—then I'm way sicker than I thought.

To my surprise, I burst out laughing.

"That's it, Michael. Just let it out."

My laughter grows steadily louder and more hysterical, and then gradually it transitions into gut-wrenching sobs that convulse my entire body and weaken my knees until I collapse and crumple to the sidewalk. I lie there in a puddle for who knows how long, feeling utterly numb. Lamia sits by my side, strokes my hair, and murmurs that it will be all right.

Eventually I manage to get to my feet, blow my nose, and take a few deep breaths of sea air. "On the plus side," I say, "since I no longer need to worry about harming Gemma, there's nothing left to keep me from killing myself."

"Precisely," says Lamia, without a trace of levity.

Which makes me wonder why she chose this setting to inform me that Gemma is but a figment of my overactive imagination.

"If you'll allow me to recap," I say. "While perched atop Seppuku Bridge—from which two or three dozen depressives plummet to their deaths each year—I inform you that if it weren't for my beloved sister, I'd kill myself. In response, you strip me of my sole reason for living. Is that about right, Lamia, or is that, too, the product of my malignant gray matter?"

"No, that's it in a nutshell. I realize that this may appear sadistic, but I'm convinced that for you to construct a truly satisfying ending to *Incognolio*, you must fully inhabit the mind of a jumper, someone willing to plunge two hundred feet and then slam into a wall of water at seventy-five miles per hour, just to escape this vale of tears."

"But you're ignoring the fact that it's possible to *survive* the fall," I point out. "Hell, I could end up paralyzed, trapped in an inanimate body for the remainder of my pathetic existence."

"It's true that there's a survival rate of nearly three percent," Lamia admits. "But you can improve your odds of dying by assuming the optimal landing position."

"Optimal landing position? Jesus, Lamia, did you edit the fucking *Idiot's Guide to Suicide*?"

"No, but as an editor, I make it my business to avail myself of knowledge on a broad range of topics. Now, if you dive head first, you may very well survive the fall, but you'll probably drown, since you're likely to plunge seventy feet or more underwater."

"Good to know."

"And if you decide on the way down that jumping was a big mistake, then you probably want to enter the water feet first, and at a slight backward angle. Not only will this limit how far you'll sink, it'll protect your head, neck, and vital organs."

"Vital information."

"But if you *truly* want lights out, the optimal landing position is the belly flop."

"Ah, the good ol' belly flop," I say. "All righty, then. Can we go now?"

"We're not quite finished."

"Not finished? With *what?*" I'm nearly shouting at her. "I'm not jumping!"

"Of course not, Michael." Lamia's voice is calm, her tone condescending, as if she were addressing a young child. "But to write this last scene the way it must be written, you need to *be* a jumper. That's why I'd like you to climb over the railing and briefly stand on the other side, facing the water."

"Are you out of your fucking mind?"

"As your editor, I'm just trying—"

"Forget the damn novel. You've taken away my one reason for living. Why would I give a shit about whether the novel gets published?"

"Don't you want *some* sort of legacy?" Lamia's gaze probes mine until I'm forced to hang my head. "You dropped out of high school and never held a job for more than a month. Wrote obsessively, but failed to publish anything. Never had a girlfriend, Michael, let alone a child. Living off a trust fund since your mom died. What the hell do you have to show for this pitiful excuse for a life? Christ, you don't even have Yiddle to take pride in anymore."

My poor, sweet bird. African grey parrots can live to be sixty or older, but Yiddle expired at age thirty while playing around with my damned Dustbuster. The final *fuck you* from an indifferent—possibly malevolent—universe.

CHAPTER FORTY-FOUR

THE HUMAN EXTINCTION FUND

Well, I can hardly dispute Lamia's grim synopsis of my time upon this Earth.

And to be honest, I *would* like to leave some sort of legacy, even if it's just the literary equivalent of shouting *fuck you* back at the universe.

I also find myself agreeing with Lamia that jumping off a bridge provides the perfect ending to my novel. Having the Author fall to his death carries a whiff of inevitability and reverberates with several other falls: Muldoon toppling down Bottomless Boulevard in his attempt to escape the snarling gargoyles; the young Micaela plunging to her death from the Ferris wheel gondola; Misha's experience during the Wakan ceremony of falling through the Earth and deep into space; and Muldoon leaping from the sixth floor of the Literary Arts Building into the void to find the Goddess.

Now that I think about it, when I began writing *Incognolio*, with no clue as to where the story was headed, that too felt like a leap into the unknown.

"Fine, I'll finish the manuscript," I tell Lamia. "But I'm not sticking around to get it published."

"I'll take care of that, cuz, and I'll do it for free. Where would you like me to donate the royalties?"

"The Human Extinction Fund."

"Worthy cause."

Like the true madman I now know myself to be, I start to climb over the railing I've been clinging to. Then I halt, with one leg on either side of the iron bar. "I'm not doing this," I tell Lamia, "unless you stand at least ten paces away from me."

"No problem." She complies with my request. "Afraid I'll push you, huh?"

"It crossed my mind."

"And what motive do you imagine would drive me to kill my dear cousin?"

"You told me that you loved my novel." I lift my other leg over the railing and then lower myself about eighteen inches until I'm standing on a narrow ledge with my back to the bay. "Perhaps you'd like to publish it under your own name."

"Scores of agents know you wrote it," Lamia replies. "I could never get away with passing it off as mine."

"Or maybe you're sick of the responsibilities associated with guardianship and wish to hasten my departure from this blighted planet."

"It appears we've entered the State of Paranoia, so allow me to join in on the fun." Lamia takes a step toward me, but my scowl sends her scurrying right back. "Maybe I wanna rub you out before you murder me, like you habitually tried to kill Gemma."

"Hilarious," I say, and then it occurs to me. "Hey, wait a minute! If Gemma isn't real, then she never confided in you, so how do you know about my attempts to waste her?"

Disconcerted by this apparent hole in her narrative, I start to climb back to safety, but Lamia tells me to wait.

"When your father took off, Michael, your mom became the sole parent of a highly disturbed toddler. Socially isolated, she turned to her sister—my mother, Fallopia—for support. In turn, my mom filled me in on all your antics, including your attempts on Gemma's life."

"Oh," I say, and climb back down onto the ledge. Dispirited, I slowly turn around until I'm facing the water, my arms spread out like the crucified Christ, hands clutching the railing.

"Okay, now listen only to the sound of my voice," says Lamia in a hypnotic tone. "I'd like you to dwell on everything you hate about your life, Michael. Let your worst memories, your most painful experiences, your crushed dreams, flood your awareness. Stand toe-to-toe with all of the misery, guilt, rage, self-hatred, and despair that you've ever tried to fend off with alcohol, masturbation, writing, and dark humor."

"Jesus, Lamia. What the fuck is this? Affirmations from Hell?"

"I'm simply trying to usher you into an appropriate mindset. The best way I've discovered to do that is to ruminate on the shittiest aspects of your life, to become aware of how you wish you were never born, and to yearn for the sweet oblivion that preceded your birth."

"Now, you listen to *me*," I say. Still clutching the railing with both hands, I twist around to address Lamia. "I don't need a goddamn tutorial in feeling suicidal, from you or anybody else. Believe me, when it comes to—"

Suddenly my right foot slips off the ledge, followed quickly by my left. The jolt pries my hand loose from the railing, and before I know it, I'm dangling in mid-air by my left hand like a chimpanzee.

Too panicked to form words, I settle for yelping.

Lamia leans over and reaches for my free hand. When she grasps it, she swings me around so that I'm facing her and tells me to step back onto the ledge.

I manage to do so, my entire body trembling, my breathing labored. Lamia continues to grip my sweaty palms and peers into my eyes, our faces just inches apart.

"So, you want to live?" Lamia asks.

I nod, still catching my breath.

Lamia continues to hold my hands, and I have the distinct sense that she revels in wielding power over me. Eager to return to solid ground, I reach with both hands for the railing, but my cousin—whose strength surprises me—resists my efforts, keeping my hands immobilized.

"What are you doing?" I ask. "I'm ready to climb back up."

"I'm afraid that's not part of the plan," she replies, and that crooked grin reappears.

Before I can ask what plan she's referring to, a figure emerges from the fog and plants a kiss on Lamia's cheek.

"*Gemma!*" I shout. "What the *fuck?*"

Gemma briefly caresses Lamia's butt. "Nice job, babe. I *told* you he's a dimwit."

Truth be told, I do feel foolish for letting Lamia convince me that my twin died at birth, and that my imagination conjured up Gemma.

The two women silently regard me. I'm struck by their beauty, and by the iciness of their gazes.

"What the hell is going on?" I say.

"We knew we'd never get you out on that ledge unless you believed I didn't exist," says Gemma, as she slides over and takes my hands from Lamia. "We just never dreamed it would be so easy to gaslight you."

"But isn't your strategy a bit extreme?" I ask. "Hey, I can move out tomorrow, Gem. You'll never hear from me again."

"Bullshit." Gemma's eyes are wild. "You're a bloodsucker, Michael. A relentless parasite who feeds off my life energy and won't ever let go. Now I can finally exterminate you, and it'll look like suicide."

"I can change, I swear."

"You've been saying that since you hit puberty. But you *don't* change, do you? I work full time, and yet you never help out with the cooking or cleaning. You contribute nothing to the household, and yet you feel entitled to being pampered. When was the last time you even put the damn toilet seat down?"

I'm formulating my rebuttal when my sister resumes her tirade.

"You have stubbornly refused to accept a platonic relationship. When your begging fails and your seductions fall flat, you paw me in my sleep, or get me drunk to the point of passing out."

"I have *never* pulled a Cosby," I say, doing my best to sound offended.

"And when you're not trying to fuck me, you're scheming to kill me. Just last week you threw an iron into my goddamn bathwater."

"Hey, it was set on *Spandex*, for shit's sake. If you hadn't been using Epsom salts you would've barely been singed."

"See? He's *always* got an excuse," Gemma complains to Lamia. "I should have left the bastard *decades* ago. Instead, I hung in there, thinking that with enough love and patience I could bring him around. But I refuse to play the martyr any longer."

"You've got to believe me, Gem," I plead. "This bridge experience has been transformational. I *can* change. I'll be less selfish. Shift the focus from my own trivial concerns to helping other folks. Overcome my anxieties and engage with the world. Maybe even start leaving the house. Just give me *one* last chance. It'll be like when we were kids. Like back in the womb."

"We can never live in harmony again, Michael, and you know it. You're far too threatened by your feminine side. You killed me off at birth in your novel, and you keep trying to destroy me in real life. Now *I'm* ready to be rid of *you*."

"And shack up with Lamia?"

"That's none of your business," Gemma replies. "But, yes, we're lovers. Have been for years."

"As were our mothers," Lamia adds. "In case you failed to notice."

Ignoring Lamia's ridiculous assertion, I say, "I'm in the way, I get that. Fine, I'll clear out. There's no need to annihilate me."

"I don't trust you," Gemma replies. "You'll find some way to undermine us, to exact your revenge. But the Age of Man has come to an end, my dear brother, and I'm afraid you're the fall guy."

And with that, Gemma pushes me, knocking my feet off the ledge and sending me plunging downward.

CHAPTER FORTY-FIVE

DESCENT OF MAN

Plummeting toward the bay at an alarming rate of speed, I take dubious solace in the fact that my life isn't flashing before my eyes.

Midway through the fall, however, another quirky response of the human-brain-in-mortal-danger kicks in: My sense of time slows, stretching out until I barely seem to be moving at all.

My first thought is that, although I'm not looking forward to the moment of impact, I can't say that I'm entirely unhappy with this turn of events.

Still, I wish that I'd been able to drag Gem and Lamia down with me. The image of my sister and that miscreant living together in lesbian bliss—laughing, drinking, frolicking, fucking—makes me want to puke, but that would only aggravate my current predicament.

But no matter how much I loathe my cousin, I can't deny that this fall would have made a far more dramatic ending to *Incognolio* than the one I wrote.

This thought leads me to wonder whether Lamia will try to publish my manuscript. But I don't see how she could use this improved ending, since it would implicate her and Gemma in my disappearance. And now it occurs to me that her glowing praise might have been insincere—merely a ruse to gain my cooperation so she could lure me to my death—a thought that extinguishes my pride in the novel, thus ripping away my final remaining illusion.

As I continue to fall, I find that I can shift my body around, so I start to weigh the various options for landing. Diving position is out, since I could survive the fall only to asphyxiate on the way back up to the surface, and I can hardly imagine a worse way of dying than to drown. The idea of a 75-mile-per-hour belly flop is horrifying, to state the obvious, but at least this "optimal landing position" would ensure instantaneous death.

However, I cannot deny that a small—but rapidly expanding—part of me wants to live, if only to thwart Gem and Lamia and to exact sweet revenge upon those scheming whores. The problem is, I can't swim, or even tread water, which means that any sort of rescue would be extremely un—

The front door slams, jolting me out of my narrative.

Frame-break! squawks Yiddle, alive and well, perched atop a bust of Cervantes.

I look up from the screen and call out, "Is that you, sweetie?" even though I've got no idea to whom I'm speaking.

Hearing footsteps approaching, I decide that it's Luna, my wife, just home from work. She storms into my study, wearing nothing but a scowl on her face.

"What the hell?" I stand up to greet her. "Why are you naked?"

"Forgot already?" Luna shrugs me off when I try to hug her. "This was my nip day."

Nip day! *Nip day*! squawks Yiddle.

"Your *what*? Jesus, Luna, have you gone back to drinking nips? You *know* how alcohol affects you."

"No, you idiot. NIP! Naked In Public Day. Remember? Trump's lottery?"

I have no idea what she's talking about. But then I remember—or do I decide?—that when he realized that a second term was beyond his grasp, Trump declared the United States a monarchy, and as king, one of his first royal decrees was to establish Naked In Public Days. As determined by an annual lottery linked to birth date, all females between the ages of sixteen and thirty-five must spend one day completely nude in public.

"It was a nightmare, Calvino." Luna now accepts a hug as she starts to sob. "Catcalls. Pinching. Ass-slapping. Men—even *boys*—pawing me, licking me, kicking me, spitting at me. I want to die."

I stroke Luna's hair, still sticky from dried layers of saliva, and soothe my wife until her weeping subsides.

"Calvino?" I repeat.

"Huh?"

"You called me Calvino. Is that some sort of pet name?"

Luna steps back and looks at me like I've gone nuts.

"Pet name? That *is* your name. Calvino Lazar."

Reverse pen name! squawks Yiddle.

Calvino Lazar. I like the sound of it. But how can that be my name? "My name is Michael," I say. "Michael Sussman."

"Are you feeling all right?" Luna frowns and then places the back of her hand against my forehead. "Michael is the protagonist of your novel, *Incognolio Zlatch*."

"Zlatch?" I feel weak. The room starts to spin. "What the hell is a zlatch?"

"I think you'd better lie down, Cal." Luna, who has just experienced the worst day of her life, leads me by my hand to our bedroom.

"Here we go." She helps me down and slips off my shoes. "I'll brew you some moochi."

"Moochi?" I repeat, my own voice sounding strange.

Luna shakes her head, looking like someone whose husband has succumbed to early dementia, and shuffles out of the room. I feel bereft, a stranger in a strange land of my own design. I start to cry, but quickly gather myself when I hear Luna returning. She has donned a kimono and wrapped her hair in a towel.

"So, let me get this straight." I blow on the moochi, which is steaming hot. "My name is Calvino Lazar, the author of *Incognolio Zlatch*. My novel features a protagonist named Michael Sussman who wrote an unpublished novel called *Incognolio*, and is currently falling to his death."

"Oh, he's still falling?" Luna retrieves a crazy quilt from the closet. "I thought he would've reached bottom by now. Wasn't he falling when I left this morning?"

"Yeah, but I've never fallen a long distance, so I had to do some research to nail the scene."

"What sort of research?" Luna spreads the quilt over the lower half of my body.

"I went bungee jumping," I say, recalling the sensation of falling—at once thrilling and terrifying, with my breath stuck in my throat and heart racing, I'd never felt so alive. I take a sip of moochi, which tastes like bumble bees. "Off the Seppuku Bridge."

"The Seppuku Bridge?" Luna tilts her head like a dog. "But you made that up. That's a bridge in *Michael's* world."

"Is it?" I take another sip of moochi, wondering how it could possibly taste like bumble bees. "Anyhoo. Freefall felt flabulous. So great, infarct, that I booked a ride on a Zorro-gravity plane."

"Zero," says Luna.

"Huh?"

"*Zero*-gravity plane. You said Zorro."

"I did?" Something seems to be curdling my brine, and I wonder weather it's the moochi or the crazy quilt. "Well, that made me wait less, which was fun. But it's nothing like freefall. So, I signed up to go skydiving."

"You did all this *today?*" asks Luna.

"Time is subjunctive," I reply. "It slurs and leaches when you're falling to your deaf."

"Hold on. It's *Michael* who's falling to his death, not you."

Such distinctions seem bestride the point this late in the gnome, so I ignore Ms. Lunatic.

"Well, my first dive had to be tandem, and though I thinks meself open-wounded, I wasn't wild about having some duderonomy riding my ass for ten thousand feets. So, instead, I rented a wingsuit."

"A wingsuit? Are you nuts?" Lorna picks up the fone, no doubt planning to have me commiserated. "People get killed on those jumps."

"Specially when yer group includes two loverly twins on their nip day."

"So you knew all along about nip day! Why did you act like—"

"I stood alone on the clift after everyone else had humped," I say, ignoring Lunesta's attempt to tractor me. "It was so froggy that I couldn't even see the drop zone. Kneading to gnaw what it's like to fall without hope of survival, I planned to deploy my parakeet at the last possible Sanka. But as I stood there looking down, feeling immortalized, yearning to make the leap, but faced with the fucked that I'm—"

Emerging from my daydream, I feel myself picking up speed once more and suddenly break through the fog bank, the bay charging up at me like a wall of doom.

As the end approaches, the rushing air drowns out my thoughts, leaving only an enormous relief at no longer feeling burdened by petty concerns of life and death. And as I surrender myself to the void and bid welcome to sweet oblivion, I hear the most delightful of sounds, a sound that is more resplendent than any human song, a sound that can only be the voice of the Goddess Herself, beckoning me to Eden, to Eternal Bliss…or perhaps—I find myself pondering as my consciousness is snuffed out—it could simply be a foghorn.

INCOGNOLIO ZLATCH

a novel by

CALVINO LAZAR

as told to
Michael Sussman

ABOUT THE
AUTHOR

Abandoned by a cackle of laughing hyenas, Michael Sussman endured the drudgery and hardships of a Moldavian orphanage until fleeing with a traveling circus at the age of twelve. A promising career as a trapeze artist was cut short by a concussion that rendered him lame and mute. Sussman wandered the world, getting by on such odd jobs as pet-food tester, cheese sculptor, human scarecrow, and professional mourner while teaching himself the art of fiction. He now lives in Tahiti with Gauguin, an African Grey parrot.